Everyman

BOOKS BY PHILIP ROTH

ZUCKERMAN BOOKS

The Ghost Writer
Zuckerman Unbound
The Anatomy Lesson
The Prague Orgy

The Counterlife

American Pastoral
I Married a Communist
The Human Stain

ROTH BOOKS

The Facts · Deception
Patrimony · Operation Shylock
The Plot Against America

KEPESH BOOKS

The Breast
The Professor of Desire
The Dying Animal

MISCELLANY

Reading Myself and Others
Shop Talk

OTHER BOOKS

Goodbye, Columbus · Letting Go
When She Was Good · Portnoy's Complaint · Our Gang
The Great American Novel · My Life as a Man
Sabbath's Theater · Everyman

Everyman

Philip Roth

Houghton Mifflin Company

BOSTON · NEW YORK

2006

For information about permission to reproduce selections
from this book, write to Permissions, Houghton Mifflin Company,
215 Park Avenue South, New York, New York 10003.

ISBN-13: 978-0-7394-7579-9

Printed in the United States of America

Book design by Robert Overholtzer

To J. C.

Here, where men sit and hear each other groan;
Where palsy shakes a few, sad, last grey hairs,
Where youth grows pale, and spectre-thin, and dies;
Where but to think is to be full of sorrow . . .

—JOHN KEATS, "Ode to a Nightingale"

Around the grave in the rundown cemetery were a few of his former advertising colleagues from New York, who recalled his energy and originality and told his daughter, Nancy, what a pleasure it had been to work with him. There were also people who'd driven up from Starfish Beach, the residential retirement village at the Jersey Shore where he'd been living since Thanksgiving of 2001—the elderly to whom only recently he'd been giving art classes. And there were his two sons, Randy and Lonny, middle-aged men from his turbulent first marriage, very much their mother's children, who as a consequence knew little of him that was praiseworthy and much that was beastly and who were present out of duty and nothing more. His older brother, Howie, and his sister-in-law were there, having flown in from California the night before, and there was one of his three ex-wives, the middle one, Nancy's mother, Phoebe, a tall, very thin white-haired woman whose right arm hung limply at her side. When asked by Nancy if she wanted to say anything, Phoebe shyly shook her head but then went ahead to speak in a soft voice, her speech faintly slurred. "It's just so hard to believe. I keep thinking of him swimming the bay—that's all. I just keep seeing him swimming the bay." And then Nancy, who had made her father's funeral arrangements and placed the phone calls to those who'd showed up so that the mourners wouldn't consist of just her mother, herself, and his brother and sister-in-law. There was only one person whose presence hadn't to do with having been invited, a heavyset woman with a pleasant round face and dyed red hair who had simply appeared at the cemetery and introduced herself as Maureen, the private duty nurse who had looked after him following his heart surgery years back. Howie remembered her and went up to kiss her cheek.

Nancy told everyone, "I can begin by saying something to you about this cemetery, because I've discovered that my father's grandfather, my great-grandfather, is not only buried in the original few acres alongside my great-grandmother but was one of its founders in 1888. The association that first financed and erected the cemetery was composed of the burial societies of Jewish benevolent organizations and congregations scattered across Union and Essex counties. My great-grandfather owned and ran a boarding house in Elizabeth that catered especially to newly arrived immigrants, and he was concerned with their well-being as more than a mere landlord. That's why he was among the original members who purchased the open field that was here and who themselves graded and landscaped it, and why he served as the first cemetery chairman. He was relatively young then but in his full vigor, and it's his name alone that is signed to the document specifying that the cemetery was for 'burying deceased members in accordance with Jewish law and ritual.' As is all too obvious, the maintenance of individual plots and of the fencing and the gates is no longer what it should be. Things have rotted and toppled over, the gates are rusted, the locks are gone, there's been vandalism. By now the place has become the butt end of the airport and what you're hearing from a few miles away is the steady din of the New Jersey Turnpike. Of course I thought first of the truly beautiful places where my father might be buried, the places where he and my mother used to swim together when they were young, and the places where he loved to swim at the shore. Yet despite the fact that looking around at the deterioration here breaks my heart—as it probably does yours, and perhaps even makes you wonder why we're assembled on grounds so badly scarred by time —I wanted him to lie close to those who loved him and from whom he descended. My father loved his parents and he should be near them. I didn't want him to be somewhere alone." She was silent for a moment to collect herself. A gentle-faced woman in her mid-thirties, plainly pretty as her mother had been, she looked all at once in no way authoritative or even brave but like a ten-year-old overwhelmed. Turning toward the coffin, she picked up a clod of dirt and, before dropping it onto the lid, said lightly, with the air still of a bewildered young girl, "Well, this is how it turns out. There's nothing more we can do, Dad." Then she remembered his own stoical maxim from decades back and began to cry.

"There's no remaking reality," she told him. "Just take it as it comes. Hold your ground and take it as it comes."

The next to throw dirt onto the lid of the coffin was Howie, who'd been the object of his worship when they were children and in return had always treated him with gentleness and affection, patiently teaching him to ride a bike and to swim and to play all the sports in which Howie himself excelled. It still appeared as if he could run a football through the middle of the line, and he was seventy-seven years old. He'd never been hospitalized for anything and, though a sibling bred of the same stock, had remained triumphantly healthy all his life.

His voice was husky with emotion when he whispered to his wife, "My kid brother. It makes no sense." Then he too addressed everyone. "Let's see if I can do it. Now let's get to this guy. About my brother . . ." He paused to compose his thoughts so that he could speak sensibly. His way of talking and the pleasant pitch of his voice were so like his brother's that Phoebe began to cry, and, quickly, Nancy took her by the arm. "His last few years," he said, gazing toward the grave, "he had health problems, and there was also loneliness—no less a problem.

We spoke on the phone whenever we could, though near the end of his life he cut himself off from me for reasons that were never clear. From the time he was in high school he had an irresistible urge to paint, and after he retired from advertising, where he'd made a considerable success first as an art director and then when he was promoted to be a creative director—after a life in advertising he painted practically every day of every year that was left to him. We can say of him what has doubtless been said by their loved ones about nearly everyone who is buried here: he should have lived longer. He should have indeed." Here, after a moment's silence, the resigned look of gloom on his face gave way to a sorrowful smile. "When I started high school and had team practice in the afternoons, he took over the errands that I used to run for my father after school. He loved being only nine years old and carrying the diamonds in an envelope in his jacket pocket onto the bus to Newark, where the setter and the sizer and the polisher and the watch repairman our father used each sat in a cubbyhole of his own, tucked away on Frelinghuysen Avenue. Those trips gave that kid enormous pleasure. I think watching these artisans doing their lonely work in those tight little places gave him the idea for using his hands to make art. I think looking at the facets of the diamonds through my father's jewelry loupe is something else that fostered his desire to make art." A laugh suddenly got the upper hand with Howie, a little flurry of relief from his task, and he said, "I was the conventional brother. In me diamonds fostered a desire to make money." Then he resumed where he'd left off, looking through the large sunny window of their boyhood years. "Our father took a small ad in the *Elizabeth Journal* once a month. During the holiday season, between Thanksgiving and Christmas, he took the ad once a week. 'Trade in your old watch for a new one.' All these old watches that he accumulated—most of them beyond repair—were dumped in a drawer in the back of the store. My little brother could sit there for hours, spinning the hands and listening to the watches tick, if they still did, and studying what each face and what each case looked like. That's what made that *boy* tick. A hundred, two hundred trade-in watches, the entire drawerful probably worth no more than ten bucks, but to his budding artist's eye, that backroom watch drawer was a treasure chest. He used to take them and wear them—he always had a watch that was out of that drawer. One of the ones that worked. And the ones he tried to make work, whose looks he liked, he'd fiddle around with but to no avail—generally he'd only make them worse. Still, that was the beginning of his using his hands to perform meticulous tasks. My father always had two girls just out of high school, in their late teens or early twenties, helping him behind the counter in the store. Nice, sweet Elizabeth girls, well-mannered, clean-cut girls, always Christian, mainly Irish Catholic, whose fathers and brothers and uncles worked for Singer Sewing Machine or for the biscuit company or down at the port. He figured nice Christian girls would make the customers feel more at home. If asked to, the girls would try on the jewelry for the customers, model it for them, and if we were lucky, the women would wind up buying. As my father told us, when a pretty young woman wears a piece of jewelry, other women think that when they wear the piece of jewelry they'll look like that too. The guys off the docks at the port who came in looking for engagement rings and wedding rings for their girlfriends would sometimes have the temerity to take the salesgirl's hand in order to examine the stone up close. My brother liked to be around the girls too, and that was long before he could even begin to understand what it was he was enjoying so much. He would help the girls empty the window and the showcases at the end of the day. He'd do anything at all to help them. They'd empty the windows and cases of everything but the cheapest stuff, and just before closing time this little kid would open the big safe in the backroom with the combination my father had entrusted to him. I'd done all these jobs before him, including getting as close as I could to the girls, especially to two blond sisters named Harriet and May. Over the years there was Harriet, May, Annmarie, Jean, there was Myra, Mary, Patty, there was Kathleen and Corine, and every one of them took a shine to that kid. Corine, the great beauty, would sit at the workbench in the backroom in early November and she and my kid brother would address the catalogues the store printed up and sent to all the customers for the holiday buying season, when my father was open six nights a week and everybody worked like a dog. If you gave my brother a box of envelopes, he could count them faster than anybody because his fingers were so dexterous and because he counted the envelopes by fives. I'd look in and, sure enough, that's what he'd be doing—showing off with the envelopes for Corine. How that boy loved doing everything that went along with being the jeweler's reliable son! That was our father's favorite accolade —'reliable.' Over the years our father sold wedding rings to Elizabeth's Irish and Germans and Slovaks and Italians and Poles, most of them young working-class stiffs. Half the time, after he'd made the sale, we'd be invited, the whole family, to the wedding. People liked him—he had a sense of humor and he kept his prices low and he extended credit to everyone, so we'd go—first to the church, then on to the noisy festivities. There was the Depression, there was the war, but there were also the weddings, there were our salesgirls, there were the trips to Newark on the bus with hundreds of dollars' worth of diamonds stashed away in envelopes in the pockets of our mackinaws. On the outside of each envelope were the instructions for the setter or the sizer written by our father. There was the five-foot-high Mosley safe slotted for all the jewelry trays that we carefully put away every night and removed every morning . . . and all of this constituted the core of my brother's life as a good little boy." Howie's eyes rested on the coffin again. "And now what?" he asked. "I think this had better be all there is. Going on and on, remembering still more . . . but why not remember? What's another gallon of tears between family and friends? When our father died my brother asked me if I minded if he took our father's watch. It was a Hamilton, made in Lancaster, P-A, and according to the expert, the boss, the best watch this country ever produced. Whenever he sold one, our father never failed to assure the customer that he'd made no mistake. 'See, I wear one myself. A very, very highly respected watch, the Hamilton. To my mind,' he'd say, 'the premier American-made watch, bar none.' Seventy-nine fifty, if I remember correctly. Everything for sale in those days had to end in fifty. Hamilton had a great reputation. It *was* a classy watch, my dad did love his, and when my brother said he'd like to own it, I couldn't have been happier. He could have taken the jeweler's loupe and our father's diamond carrying case. That was the worn old leather case that he would always carry with him in his coat pocket whenever he went to do business outside the store:

with the tweezers in it, and the tiny screwdrivers and the little ring of sizers that gauge the size of a round stone and the folded white papers for holding the loose diamonds. The beautiful, cherished little things he worked with, which he held in his hands and next to his heart, yet we decided to bury the loupe and the case and all its contents in his grave. He always kept the loupe in one pocket and his cigarettes in the other, so we stuck the loupe inside his shroud. I remember my brother saying, 'By all rights we should put it in his eye.' That's what grief can do to you. That's how thrown we were. We didn't know what else to do. Rightly or wrongly, there didn't seem to us anything but that to do. Because they were not just his—they were *him* . . . To finish up about the Hamilton, my father's old Hamilton with the crown that you would turn to wind it every morning and that you would pull out on its stem to turn to move the hands . . . except while he was in swimming, my brother wore it day and night. He took it off for good only forty-eight hours ago. He handed it to the nurse to lock away for safekeeping while he was having the surgery that killed him. In the car on the way to the cemetery this morning, my niece Nancy showed me that she'd put a new notch in the band and now it's she who's wearing the Hamilton to tell time by."

Then came the sons, men in their late forties and looking, with their glossy black hair and their eloquent dark eyes and the sensual fullness of their wide, identical mouths, just like their father (and like their uncle) at their age. Handsome men beginning to grow beefy and seemingly as closely linked with each other as they'd been irreconcilably alienated from the dead father. The younger, Lonny, stepped up to the grave first. But once he'd taken a clod of dirt in his hand, his entire body began to tremble and quake, and it looked as though he were on the edge of violently regurgitating. He was overcome with a feeling for his father that wasn't antagonism but that his antagonism denied him the means to release. When he opened his mouth, nothing emerged except a series of grotesque gasps, making it appear likely that whatever had him in its grip would never be finished with him. He was in so desperate a state that Randy, the older, more decisive son, the scolding son, came instantly to his rescue. He took the clod of dirt from the hand of the younger one and tossed it onto the casket for both of them. And he readily met with success when he went to speak. "Sleep easy, Pop," Randy said, but any note of tenderness, grief, love, or loss was terrifyingly absent from his voice.

The last to approach the coffin was the private duty nurse, Maureen, a battler from the look of her and no stranger to either life or death. When, with a smile, she let the dirt slip slowly across her curled palm and out the side of her hand onto the coffin, the gesture looked like the prelude to a carnal act. Clearly this was a man to whom she'd once given much thought.

That was the end. No special point had been made. Did they all say what they had to say? No, they didn't, and of course they did. Up and down the state that day, there'd been five hundred funerals like his, routine, ordinary, and except for the thirty wayward seconds furnished by the sons—and Howie's resurrecting with such painstaking precision the world as it innocently existed before the invention of death, life perpetual in their father-created Eden, a paradise just fifteen feet wide by forty feet deep disguised as an old-style jewelry store —no more or less interesting than any of the others. But then it's the commonness that's most wrenching, the registering once more of the fact of death that overwhelms everything.

In a matter of minutes, everybody had walked away—wearily and tearfully walked away from our species' least favorite activity—and he was left behind. Of course, as when anyone dies, though many were grief-stricken, others remained unperturbed, or found themselves relieved, or, for reasons good or bad, were genuinely pleased.

Though he had grown accustomed to being on his own and fending for himself since his last divorce ten years back, in his bed the night before the surgery he worked at remembering as exactly as he could each of the women who had been there waiting for him to rise out of the anesthetic in the recovery room, even remembering that most helpless of mates, the last wife, with whom recovering from quintuple bypass surgery had not been a sublime experience. The sublime experience had been the private nurse with the unassuming professional air who'd come home with him from the hospital and who tended him with a high-spirited devotion that promoted a slow, steady recovery and with whom, unknown to his wife, he conducted a sustained affair once he had recovered his sexual prowess. Maureen. Maureen Mrazek. He'd called all over trying to find Maureen. He'd wanted her to come and be his nurse, should he need a nurse, when he got home from the hospital this time. But sixteen years had passed, and the nursing agency at the hospital had lost track of her. She'd be forty-eight now, more than likely married and a mother, a shapely, energetic young woman grown into middle-aged stoutness while the battle to remain an unassailable man had by then been lost by him, time having transformed his own body into a storehouse for manmade contraptions designed to fend off collapse. Defusing thoughts of his own demise had never required more diligence and cunning.

A lifetime later, he remembered the trip to the hospital with his mother for his hernia operation in the fall of 1942, a bus ride lasting no more than ten minutes. Usually if he was traveling somewhere with his mother, it was in the family car and his father was driving. But now there were just the two of them alone together on the bus, and they were headed for the hospital where he had been born, and she was what calmed his apprehension and allowed him to be brave. As a small child he'd had his tonsils removed at the hospital, but otherwise he'd never been back there. Now he was to stay for four days and four nights. He was a sensible boy of nine with no conspicuous problems, but on the bus he felt much younger and found that he required his mother's proximity in ways he thought he'd outgrown.

His brother, a high school freshman, was in class, and his father had driven the car to work well before he and his mother left for the hospital. A small overnight case rested on his mother's lap. In it were a toothbrush, pajamas, a bathrobe and slippers, and the books he'd brought with him to read. He could still remember which books they were. The hospital was around the corner from the local branch library, so his mother could replenish his reading material should he read through the books he'd brought for his hospital stay. He was to spend a week convalescing at home before returning to school, and he was more anxious about all the school he was missing than he was as yet about the ether mask that he knew they would clamp over his face to anesthetize him. In the early forties hospitals didn't as yet permit parents to stay overnight with their children, and so he'd be sleeping without his mother, his father, or his brother anywhere nearby. He was anxious about that, too.

His mother was well-spoken and mannerly, as, in turn, were the women who registered him at the admissions office and the nurses at the nurses' station when he and his mother made their way by elevator to the children's wing of the surgical floor. His mother took his overnight case because, small as it was, he wasn't supposed to carry anything until after his hernia was repaired and he had fully recuperated. He had discovered the swelling in his left groin a few months earlier and had told no one but just tried pressing it down with his fingers to make it go away. He did not know exactly what a hernia was or what significance to give to swelling located so close to his genitals.

In those days a doctor could prescribe a stiff corset with metal stays if the family didn't want the child to undergo surgery or if they couldn't afford it. He knew of a boy at school who wore such a corset, and one of the reasons he'd told no one about the swelling was his fear that he too would have to wear a corset and reveal it to the other boys when he changed into his shorts for gym class.

Once he had finally confessed to his parents, his

father took him to the doctor's office. Quickly the doctor examined him and made the diagnosis and, after conversing with his father for a few minutes, arranged for the surgery. Everything was done with astonishing speed, and the doctor—the very one who had delivered him into the world—assured him that he was going to be fine and then went on to joke about the comic strip *Li'l Abner*, which the two of them enjoyed reading in the evening paper.

The surgeon, Dr. Smith, was said by his parents to be the best in the city. Like the boy's own father, Dr. Smith, born Solly Smulowitz, had grown up in the slums, the son of poor immigrants.

He was in bed in his room within an hour of arriving at the hospital, though the surgery was not scheduled until the following morning—that's how patients were tended to then.

In the bed next to his was a boy who'd had stomach surgery and wasn't allowed to get up and walk yet. The boy's mother sat beside the bed holding her son's hand. When the father came to visit after work, the parents spoke in Yiddish, which made him think that they were too worried to speak understandable English in their son's presence. The only place where he heard Yiddish spoken was at the jewelry store when the war refugees came in search of Schaffhausen watches, a hard-to-find brand that his father would call around to try to locate for them—"Schaffhausen—I want a Schaffhausen," that would be the extent of their English. Of course Yiddish was spoken all but exclusively when the Hasidic Jews from New York traveled to Elizabeth once or twice a month to replenish the store's diamond inventory—for his father to have maintained a large inventory in his own safe would have been too expensive. There were far fewer Hasidic diamond merchants in America before the war than after, but his father, from the very beginning, preferred to deal with them rather than with the big diamond houses. The diamond merchant who came most frequently—and whose migration route had carried him and his family in only a few years from Warsaw to Antwerp to New York—was an older man dressed in a large black hat and a long black coat of a kind that you never saw on anyone else in Elizabeth's streets, not even other Jews. He wore a beard and sidelocks and kept the waist pouch that held his diamonds secreted beneath fringed undergarments whose religious significance eluded the nascent secularist—that, in fact, seemed ludicrous to him—even after his father explained why the Hasidim still wore what their ancestors had worn in the old country two hundred years before and lived much as they did then, though, as he pointed out to his father again and again, they were now in America, free to dress and to shave and to behave as they wished. When one of the seven sons of the diamond merchant got married, the merchant invited their entire family to the wedding in Brooklyn. All the men there had beards and all the women wore wigs and the sexes sat on different sides of the synagogue, separated by a wall—afterward the men and the women did not even dance together—and everything about that wedding he and Howie hated. When the diamond merchant arrived at the store he would remove his coat but leave on his hat, and the two men would sit behind the showcase chatting amiably together in Yiddish, the language that his father's parents, his own grandparents, had continued to speak in their immigrant households with their American-born children for as long as they lived. But when it was time to look at the diamonds, the two went into the backroom, where there was a safe and a workbench and a brown linoleum floor and, jammed together behind a door that never shut

completely even when you had successfully struggled to hook it from within, a toilet and a tiny sink.
His father always paid on the spot with a check.

After closing the store with Howie's help—pulling the lattice gate with the padlocks across the
shop's display window, switching on the burglar
alarm, and throwing all the locks on the front door
—his father showed up in his younger son's hospital room and gave him a hug.

He was there when Dr. Smith came around to
introduce himself. The surgeon was wearing a business suit rather than a white coat, and his father
jumped to his feet as soon as he saw him enter the
room. "It's Dr. Smith!" his father cried.

"So this is my patient," Dr. Smith said. "Well,"
he told him, coming to the side of the bed to take
him firmly by the shoulder, "we're going to fix that
hernia tomorrow and you'll be as good as new.
What position do you like to play?" he asked.

"End."

"Well, you're going to be back playing end before you know it. You're going to play anything you
want. You get a good night's sleep and I'll see you in
the morning."

Daring to joke with the eminent surgeon, his

father said, "And you get a good night's sleep too."

When his dinner came, his mother and father sat and talked to him as though they were all at home. They spoke quietly so as not to disturb the sick boy or his parents, who were silent now, the mother still seated beside him and the father incessantly pacing at the foot of the bed and then out into the corridor and back. The boy hadn't so much as stirred while they were there.

At five to eight a nurse stuck her head in to announce that visiting hours were over. The parents of the other boy again spoke together in Yiddish and, after the mother repeatedly kissed the boy's forehead, they left the room. The father had tears running down his face.

Then his own parents left to go home to his brother and eat a late dinner together in the kitchen without him. His mother kissed him and held him tightly to her. "You can do it, son," his father said, leaning over to kiss him as well. "It's like when I give you an errand to run on the bus or a job to do at the store. Whatever it is, you never let me down. Reliable—my two reliable boys! I pop my buttons when I think about my boys. Always, you do the work like the thorough, careful, hard-working boys you were brought up to be. Carrying precious jewels to Newark and back, quarter-carat, half-carat diamonds in your pocket, and at your age that doesn't faze you. You look to all the world like it's some junk you found in your Cracker Jacks. Well, if you can do that job, you can do this job. It's just another job of work as far as you're concerned. Do the work, finish the job, and by tomorrow the whole thing will be over. You hear the bell, you come out fighting. Right?"

"Right," the boy said.

"By the time I see you tomorrow, Dr. Smith will have fixed that thing, and that'll be the end of that."

"Right."

"My two terrific boys!"

Then they were gone and he was alone with the boy in the next bed. He reached over to his bedside table, where his mother had piled his books, and began to read *The Swiss Family Robinson*. Then he tried *Treasure Island*. Then *Kim*. Then he put his hand under the covers to look for the hernia. The swelling was gone. He knew from past experience that there were days when the swelling would temporarily subside, but this time he was sure that it had subsided for good and that he no longer needed an operation. When a nurse came by to take his temperature, he didn't know how to tell her that the hernia had disappeared and that his parents should be called to come take him home. She looked approvingly at the titles of the books he'd brought and told him that he was free to get out of bed to use the bathroom but that otherwise he should make himself comfortable reading until she returned to put out the lights. She said nothing about the other boy, who he was sure was going to die.

At first he didn't fall asleep because of his waiting for the boy to die, and then he didn't because he couldn't stop thinking of the drowned body that had washed up on the beach that past summer. It was the body of a seaman whose tanker had been torpedoed by a German U-boat. The Coast Guard beach patrol had found the body amid the oil scum and shattered cargo cases at the edge of the beach that was only a block away from the house where his family of four rented a room for a month each summer. Most days the water was clear and he didn't worry that a drowned man would collide with his bare legs as he stepped out into the low surf. But when oil from torpedoed tankers clotted the sand and caked the bottom of his feet as he crossed the beach, he was terrified of stumbling upon a corpse. Or stumbling upon a saboteur, coming ashore to work for Hitler. Armed with rifles or submachine guns and often accompanied by trained dogs, the Coast Guardsmen patrolled day and night to prevent saboteurs from landing on the miles of deserted beaches. Yet some sneaked through without detection and, along with native-born Nazi sympathizers, were known to be in ship-to-shore communication with the U-boats that prowled the East Coast shipping lanes and had been sinking ships off New Jersey since the war began. The war was closer than most people imagined, and so was the horror. His father had read that the waters of New Jersey were "the worst ship graveyard" along the entire U.S. coastline, and now, in the hospital, he couldn't get the word "graveyard" to stop tormenting him, nor could he erase from his mind that bloated dead body the Coast Guard had removed from the few inches of surf in which it lay, while he and his brother looked on from the boardwalk.

Sometime after he'd fallen asleep he heard noises in the room and awakened to see that the curtain between the two beds had been pulled to screen off the other bed and that there were doctors and nurses at work on the other side—he could see their forms moving and could hear them whispering. When one of the nurses emerged from behind the curtain, she realized that he was awake and came over to his bed and told him softly, "Go back to sleep. You have a big day tomorrow." "What's the matter?" he asked. "Nothing," she said, "we're changing his bandages. Close your eyes and go to sleep."

He was awakened early the next morning for the operation, and there was his mother, already at the hospital and smiling at him from the foot of the bed.

"Good morning, darling. How's my brave boy?"

Looking across at the other bed, he saw that it was stripped of its bedding. Nothing could have made clearer to him what had happened than the sight of the bare mattress ticking and the uncovered pillows piled in the middle of the empty bed.

"That boy died," he said. Memorable enough that he was in the hospital that young, but even more memorable that he had registered a death. The first was the bloated body, the second was this boy. During the night, when he had awakened to see the forms moving behind the curtain, he couldn't help but think, The doctors are killing him.

"I believe he was moved, sweetheart. He had to be moved to another floor."

Just then two orderlies appeared to take him to the operating room. When he was told by one of them to use the bathroom, the first thing he did when the door was closed was to check if the hernia was gone. But the swelling had come back. There was no way out of the operation now.

His mother was allowed to walk alongside the gurney only as far as the elevator that was to take him to the operating room. There the orderlies pushed him into the elevator, and it descended until it opened onto a shockingly ugly corridor that led to an operating room where Dr. Smith was wearing a surgical gown and a white mask that changed everything about him—he might not even have been Dr. Smith. He could have been someone else entirely, someone who had not grown up the son of poor immigrants named Smulowitz, someone his father knew nothing about, someone nobody knew, someone who had just wandered into the operating room and picked up a knife. In that moment of terror when they lowered the ether mask over his face as though to smother him, he could have sworn that the surgeon, whoever he was, had whispered, "Now I'm going to turn you into a girl."

The malaise began just days after his return home from a monthlong vacation as happy as any he'd known since the family vacations at the Jersey Shore before the war. He'd spent August in a semi-furnished ramshackle house on an inland road on Martha's Vineyard with the woman whose constant lover he had been for two years. Until now they'd never dared to chance living together day in and day out, and the experiment had been a joyous success, a wonderful month of swimming and hiking and of easygoing sex at all times of the day. They'd swim across a bay to a ridge of dunes where they could lie out of sight and fuck in the sunshine and then rouse themselves to slip into their suits and swim back to the beach and collect clusters of mussels off the rocks to carry home for dinner in a pail full of seawater.

The only unsettling moments were at night, when they walked along the beach together. The dark sea rolling in with its momentous thud and the sky lavish with stars made Phoebe rapturous but

frightened him. The profusion of stars told him un-
ambiguously that he was doomed to die, and the
thunder of the sea only yards away—and the night-
mare of the blackest blackness beneath the frenzy
of the water—made him want to run from the menace of oblivion to their cozy, lighted, underfur-
nished house. This was not the way he had experienced the vastness of the sea and the big night sky
while he'd served manfully in the navy just after the
Korean War—never were they the tolling bells. He
could not understand where the fear was coming
from and had to use all his strength to conceal it
from Phoebe. Why must he mistrust his life just
when he was more its master than he'd been in
years? Why should he imagine himself on the edge
of extinction when calm, straightforward thinking
told him that there was so much more solid life to
come? Yet it happened every night during their seaside walk beneath the stars. He was not flamboyant
or deformed or extreme in any way, so why then, at
his age, should he be haunted by thoughts of dying?
He was reasonable and kindly, an amicable, moder-
ate, industrious man, as everyone who knew him
well would probably agree, except, of course, for
the wife and two boys whose household he'd left

and who, understandably, could not equate reason-
ableness and kindliness with his finally giving up on
a failed marriage and looking elsewhere for the in-
timacy with a woman that he craved.

Most people, he believed, would have thought of
him as square. As a young man, he'd thought of
himself as square, so conventional and unadventur-
ous that after art school, instead of striking out on
his own to paint and to live on whatever money he
could pick up at odd jobs—which was his secret
ambition—he was too much the good boy, and, answering to his parents' wishes rather than his own,
he married, had children, and went into advertising
to make a secure living. He never thought of himself as anything more than an average human being,
and one who would have given anything for his
marriage to have lasted a lifetime. He had married
with just that expectation. But instead marriage became his prison cell, and so, after much tortuous
thinking that preoccupied him while he worked and
when he should have been sleeping, he began fit-
fully, agonizingly, to tunnel his way out. Isn't that
what an average human being would do? Isn't that
what average human beings do every day? Contrary
to what his wife told everyone, he hadn't hungered

after the wanton freedom to do anything and everything. Far from it. He hungered for something stable all the while he detested what he had. He was not a man who wished to live two lives. He held no grudge against either the limitations or the comforts of conformity. He'd wanted merely to empty his mind of all the ugly thoughts spawned by the disgrace of prolonged marital warfare. He was not claiming to be exceptional. Only vulnerable and assailable and confused. And convinced of his right, as an average human being, to be pardoned ultimately for whatever deprivations he may have inflicted upon his innocent children in order not to live deranged half the time.

Terrifying encounters with the end? I'm thirty-four! Worry about oblivion, he told himself, when you're seventy-five! The remote future will be time enough to anguish over the ultimate catastrophe!

But no sooner did he and Phoebe return to Manhattan—where they lived in apartments some thirty blocks apart—than he mysteriously fell ill. He lost his appetite and his energy and found himself nauseated throughout the day, and he could not walk a city block without feeling weak and woozy.

The doctor could find nothing wrong with him. He had begun to see a psychoanalyst in the aftermath of his divorce, and the psychoanalyst attributed his condition to envy of a fellow art director who had just been promoted to a vice presidency in the agency.

"It makes you sick," the analyst said.

He maintained that his colleague was twelve years his senior and a generous coworker whom he only wished well, but the analyst continued to harp on "deep-seated envy" as the hidden reason for the malaise, and when circumstances proved him wrong, the analyst appeared unperturbed by his mistaken judgment.

He went to the medical doctor's office several more times in the succeeding weeks, whereas ordinarily he saw him only for a minor problem every couple of years. But he'd lost weight and the bouts of nausea were getting worse. He'd never before felt so rotten, not even after he'd left Cecilia and the two small boys and the court battle ensued over the terms of the separation and he was characterized to the court by Cecilia's attorney as "a well-known philanderer" because of the affair he was having with Phoebe, who was a new copywriter in the agency (and who was referred to in court by the plaintiff on the witness stand—aggrieved, over-wrought, as though she found herself bringing charges against the Marquis de Sade—as "number thirty-seven in his parade of girlfriends," when in fact she was looking too far into the future and Phoebe was as yet number two). At least back then there'd been a recognizable cause for all the misery he felt. But this was his turning overnight from someone who was bursting with health into someone inexplicably losing his health.

A month passed. He couldn't concentrate on his work, he gave up his morning swim, and by now he couldn't look at food. On a Friday afternoon he left work early and took a taxi to the doctor's office without having made an appointment or even a phone call. The only one he phoned was Phoebe, to tell her what he was doing.

"Admit me to a hospital," he told the doctor. "I feel like I'm dying."

The doctor made the arrangements, and Phoebe was at the hospital's information desk when he arrived. By five o'clock he was settled into a room, and just before seven a tall, tanned, good-looking middle-aged man wearing a dinner jacket came into the room and introduced himself as a surgeon who had been called by his physician to take a look at him. He was on his way to some formal event but wanted to stop by first to do a quick examination. What he did was to press his hand down very hard just above the groin on the right side. Unlike the regular physician, the surgeon kept pressing and the pain was excruciating. He felt on the verge of vomiting. The surgeon said, "Haven't you had any stomach pain before?" "No," he said. "Well, it's your appendix. You need an operation." "When?" "Now."

He saw the surgeon next in the operating room. He'd changed out of the evening clothes into a surgical gown. "You've saved me from a very boring banquet," the surgeon said.

He didn't wake up until the next morning. Standing at the foot of the bed, along with Phoebe, were his mother and father, looking grim. Phoebe, whom they did not know (other than from Cecilia's denigrating descriptions, other than from the telephone tirades ending, "I pity this Little Miss Muffet coming after me—I honestly do pity the vile little Quaker slut!"), had phoned them and they'd immediately driven over from New Jersey. As best he could make out, a male nurse seemed to be having trouble feeding some sort of tube up his nose, or maybe the nurse was trying to extract it. He spoke his first words—"Don't fuck up!"—before falling back into unconsciousness.

His mother and father were seated in chairs when he came around again. They seemed still to be tormented and weighed down by fatigue as well.

Phoebe was in a chair beside the bed holding his hand. She was a pale, pretty young woman whose soft appearance belied her equanimity and steadfastness. She manifested no fear and allowed none in her voice.

Phoebe knew plenty about physical misery because of the severe headaches that she'd dismissed as nothing back in her twenties but that she realized were migraines when they became regular and frequent in her thirties. She was lucky enough to be able to sleep when she got one, but the moment she opened her eyes, the moment she was conscious, there it was—the incredible ache on one side of her head, the pressure in her face and her jaw, and back of her eye socket a foot on her eyeball crushing it. The migraines started with spirals of light, bright spots moving in a swirl in front of her eyes even when she closed them, and then progressed to disorientation, dizziness, pain, nausea, and vomiting. "It's nothing like being in this world," she told him afterward. "There's nothing in my body but the pressure in my head." All he could do for her was to remove the big cooking pot into which she vomited, and to clean it out in the bathroom, and then to tiptoe back into the bedroom and place it beside the bed for her to use when she was sick again. For the twenty-four or forty-eight hours that the migraine lasted, she could not stand another presence in the darkened room, any more than she could bear the thinnest sliver of light filtering in from beneath the drawn shades. And no drugs helped. None of them worked for her. Once the migraine started, there was no stopping it.

"What happened?" he asked her.

"A burst appendix. You had it for some time."

"How sick am I?" he asked weakly.

"There's a lot of peritonitis. There are drains in the wound. They're draining it. You're getting big doses of antibiotics. You're going to pull through. We're going to swim across the bay again."

That was hard to believe. Back in 1943 his father

had come close to dying from undiagnosed appendicitis and severe peritonitis. He was forty-two with two young children, and he had been in the hospital—and away from his business—thirty-six days. When he got home, he was so weak he could barely make it up the one little flight to their flat, and after he'd been helped by his wife from the entryway into the bedroom, he sat on the edge of the bed, where, for the first time in the presence of his children, he broke down and cried. Eleven years earlier, his youngest brother, Sammy, the adored favorite of eight children, had died of acute appendicitis in his third year at engineering school. He was nineteen years old, having entered college at sixteen, and his ambition was to be an aeronautical engineer. Only three of the eight children had got as far as high school, and Sammy was the first and only one to go to college. His friends were the smartest boys in the neighborhood, all of them the children of Jewish immigrants who met regularly at one another's houses to play chess and to talk heatedly about politics and philosophy. He was their leader, a runner on the track team and a mathematics whiz with a sparkling personality. It was Sammy's name that his father intoned as he sobbed in the bedroom, astonished to find himself back among the family whose provider he was.

Uncle Sammy, his father, now him—the third of them to have been felled by a burst appendix and peritonitis. While he drifted in and out of consciousness for the next two days, it was not certain whether he would meet Sammy's fate or his father's.

His brother flew in from California on the second day, and when he opened his eyes and saw him at the side of the bed, a big and gentle presence, unperturbed, confident, jolly, he thought, I cannot die while Howie is here. Howie bent over to kiss his forehead, and then no sooner did he sit down in the bedside chair and take the patient's hand than time stopped, the present disappeared, and he was returned to childhood, a small boy again, preserved from worry and fear by the generous brother who slept in the bed beside his.

Howie stayed for four days. In four days he sometimes flew to Manila and Singapore and Kuala Lumpur and back. He had started at Goldman Sachs as a runner and quickly went from relaying messages to top dog on the currency-trading desk and began investing for himself in stocks. He had ended up in currency arbitrage for multinational and large foreign corporations—winemakers in France and camera makers in West Germany and automakers in Japan, for whom he turned francs and deutsche marks and yen into dollars. He traveled frequently to meet with his clients and continued investing in companies he liked, and by thirty-two he had his first million.

Sending their parents home to rest, Howie joined with Phoebe to see him through the worst of it and prepared to fly out only after receiving the doctor's assurances that the crisis was over. On the last morning, Howie quietly said to him, "You've got a good girl this time. Don't screw it up. Don't let her go."

He thought, in his joy at having survived, Was there ever a man whose appetite for life was as contagious as Howie's? Was there ever a brother as lucky as me?

He was in the hospital for thirty days. The nurses were mostly agreeable, conscientious young women with Irish accents who seemed always to have time to chat a little when they looked in on him. Phoebe came directly from work to have dinner in his room every night; he couldn't imagine what being needy and infirm like this and facing the uncanny nature of illness would have been like without her.

His brother needn't have warned him not to let her
go; he was never more determined to keep anyone.

Beyond his window he could see the leaves of
the trees turning as the October weeks went by, and
when the surgeon came around he said to him,
"When am I going to get out of here? I'm missing
the fall of 1967." The surgeon listened soberly, and
then, with a smile, he said, "Don't you get it yet?
You almost missed everything."

Twenty-two years passed. Twenty-two years of
excellent health and the boundless self-assurance
that flows from being fit—twenty-two years spared
the adversary that is illness and the calamity that
waits in the wings. As he'd reassured himself while
walking under the stars on the Vineyard with
Phoebe, he would worry about oblivion when he was
seventy-five.

He had been driving to New Jersey after work
nearly every day for over a month to see his dying
father when he wound up badly short of breath in
the City Athletic Club swimming pool one August
evening in 1989. He had gotten back from Jersey
about half an hour earlier and decided to recover

his equilibrium by taking a quick swim before heading home. Ordinarily he swam a mile at the club early each morning. He barely drank, had never smoked, and weighed precisely what he'd weighed when he got home from the navy in '57 and started his first job in advertising. He knew from the ordeal with appendicitis and peritonitis that he was as liable as anyone else to falling seriously ill, but that he, with a lifelong regimen of healthful living, would end up as a candidate for cardiac surgery seemed preposterous. It was simply not how things were going to turn out.

Yet he couldn't finish the first lap without pulling over to the side and hanging there completely breathless. He got out of the pool and sat with his legs in the water trying to calm down. He was sure that the breathlessness was the result of having seen how far his father's condition had deteriorated in just the past few days. But in fact it was his that had deteriorated, and when he went to the doctor the next morning, his EKG showed radical changes that indicated severe occlusion of his major coronary arteries. Before the day was out he was in a bed in the coronary care unit of a Manhattan hospital, having been given an angiogram that determined that surgery was essential. There were oxygen prongs in his nose and he was attached by numerous leads to a cardiac monitoring machine behind his bed. The only question was whether the surgery should take place immediately or the following morning. It was by then almost eight in the evening, and so the decision was made to wait. Sometime in the night, however, he was awakened to discover his bed surrounded by doctors and nurses, just as the bed of the boy in his room had been back when he was nine. All these years he had been alive while that boy was dead—and now he was that boy.

Some sort of medication was being administered through the IV and he vaguely understood that they were trying to avert a crisis. He could not make out what they were mumbling to one another and then he must have fallen asleep, because the next he knew it was morning and he was being rolled onto a gurney to take him to the operating room.

His wife at this time—his third and his last— bore no resemblance to Phoebe and was nothing short of a hazard in an emergency. She certainly didn't inspire confidence on the morning of the surgery, when she followed beside the gurney weeping and wringing her hands and finally, uncontrollably, cried out, "What about me?"

She was young and untried and maybe she had intended to say something different, but he took it that she meant what would happen to her should he fail to survive. "One thing at a time," he told her. "First let me die. Then I'll come help you bear up."

The operation went on for seven hours. Much of that time he was connected to a heart-lung machine that pumped his blood and breathed for him. The doctors gave him five grafts, and he emerged from the surgery with a long wound down the center of his chest and another extending from his groin to his right ankle—it was from his leg that they had removed the vein from which all but one of the grafts were fashioned.

When he came around in the recovery room there was a tube down his throat that felt as though it were going to choke him to death. Having it there was horrible, but there was no way he could communicate that to the nurse who was telling him where he was and what had happened to him. He lost consciousness then, and when he came around again the tube was still there choking him to death,

but now a nurse was explaining that it would be removed as soon as it was determined that he could
breathe on his own. Over him next was the face of
his young wife, welcoming him back to the world of
the living, where he could resume looking after her.

He had left her with a single responsibility when
he went into the hospital: to see that the car was
taken off the street where it was parked and put
into the public garage a block away. It turned out to
be a task that she was too frazzled to undertake, and
so, as he later learned, she'd had to ask one of his
friends to do it for her. He hadn't realized how observant his cardiologist was of nonmedical matters
until the man came to see him midway through his
hospital stay and told him that he could not be released from the hospital if his home care was to be
provided by his wife. "I don't like to have to say
these things, fundamentally she's not my business,
but I've watched her when she's come to visit. The
woman is basically an absence and not a presence,
and I have no choice but to protect my patient."

By this time Howie had arrived. He had flown in
from Europe, where he'd gone to do business and
also to play polo. He could ski now, skeet-shoot,
and play water polo as well as polo from atop a

pony, having acquired virtuosity in these activities in the great world long after he'd left his lower-middle-class high school in Elizabeth, where, along with the Irish-Catholic and Italian boys whose fathers worked on the docks at the port, he'd played football in the fall and pole-vaulted in the spring, all the while garnering grades good enough to earn him a scholarship to the University of Pennsylvania and then admission to the Wharton School to earn an MBA. Though his father was dying in a hospital in New Jersey and his brother recovering from open-heart surgery in a hospital in New York—and though he spent the week traveling from the one bedside to the other—Howie's vigor never lapsed, nor did his capacity to inspire confidence. The sustenance the healthy thirty-year-old wife proved incapable of providing her ailing fifty-six-year-old husband was more than compensated for by Howie's jovial support. It was Howie who suggested hiring two private duty nurses—the daytime nurse, Maureen Mrazek, and the night nurse, Olive Parrott—to substitute for the woman he'd come to refer to as "the titanically ineffective cover girl," and then he insisted, over his brother's objections, on covering the costs himself. "You were dangerously ill, you went through hell," Howie said, "and so long as I'm around, nothing and nobody is going to impede your recovery. This is just a gift to ensure the speedy restoration of your health." They were standing together by the entrance to the room. Howie spoke with his brawny arms around his brother. Much as he preferred to appear breezily superior to the claims of sentiment, his face—a virtual replica of his brother's—could not disguise his emotions when he said, "Losing Mom and Dad I have to accept. I could never accept losing you." Then he left to find the limo that was waiting downstairs to drive him to the hospital in Jersey.

Olive Parrott, the night nurse, was a large black woman whose carriage and bearing and size reminded him of Eleanor Roosevelt. Her father owned an avocado farm in Jamaica, and her mother kept a dream book in whose pages, each morning, she recorded her children's dreams. On the nights when he was too uncomfortable to sleep, Olive sat in a chair at the foot of the bed and told him innocent tales about her life as a child on the avocado farm. She had a West Indian accent and a lovely voice, and her words soothed him as no woman's had since his mother sat and talked to him in the hospital after the hernia operation. Except for the questions that he asked Olive, he remained silent, deliriously contented to be alive. It turned out that they'd caught him just in time: when he was admitted to the hospital, his coronary arteries were anywhere from ninety to ninety-five percent occluded and he'd been on the verge of a massive and probably fatal heart attack.

Maureen was a buxom, smiling redhead who had grown up something of a roughneck in an Irish-Slavic family in the Bronx and had a blunt way of talking that was fueled by the self-possession of a working-class toughie. The mere sight of her raised his spirits when she arrived in the morning, even though the postsurgical exhaustion was so severe that merely shaving—and not even shaving standing up but while sitting in a chair—tired him out, and he had to return to bed for a long nap after taking his first walk down the hospital corridor with her at his side. Maureen was the one who called his father's doctor for him and kept him informed of the dying man's condition until he had the strength to talk to the doctor himself.

It had been decided peremptorily by Howie that when he left the hospital Maureen and Olive would look after him (again at Howie's expense) for at least his first two weeks at home. His wife was not consulted, and she resented the arrangement and the implication that she was unable to care for him on her own. She particularly resented Maureen, who herself did little to hide her contempt for the patient's wife.

At home it was more than three weeks before the exhaustion began to diminish and he felt ready even to consider returning to work. After dinner he had to go back to bed for the evening simply from the effort of eating sitting up in a chair, and in the morning he had to remain seated on a plastic stool to wash himself in the shower. He began to do mild calisthenics with Maureen and tried each day to add another ten yards to the afternoon walk he took with her. Maureen had a boyfriend whom she talked about—a TV cameraman whom she expected to marry once he found a permanent job—and when she got off work at the end of the day, she liked to have a couple of drinks with the neighborhood regulars in a bar around the corner from where she lived in Yorkville. The weather was beautiful, and so when they walked outdoors he got a good look at how she carried herself in her close-fitting polo shirts and short skirts and summer sandals. Men looked her over all the time, and she was not averse to staring someone down with mock belligerence if she was being ostentatiously ogled. Her presence at his side made him feel stronger by the day, and he would come home from the walks delighted with everything, except, of course, with the jealous wife, who would slam doors and sometimes barge out of the apartment only moments after he and Maureen had swept in.

He was not the first patient to fall in love with his nurse. He was not even the first patient to fall in love with Maureen. She'd had several affairs over the years, a few of them with men rather worse off than he was, who, like him, made a full recovery with the help of Maureen's vitality. Her gift was to make the ill hopeful, so hopeful that instead of closing their eyes to blot out the world, they opened them wide to behold her vibrant presence, and were rejuvenated.

Maureen came along to New Jersey when his father died. He was still not allowed to drive, so she volunteered and helped Howie make the arrange-

ments with Kreitzer's Memorial Home in Union.
His father had become religious in the last ten
years of his life and, after having retired and having lost his wife, had taken to going to the synagogue at least once a day. Long before his final
illness, he'd asked his rabbi to conduct his burial
service entirely in Hebrew, as though Hebrew were
the strongest answer that could be accorded death.
To his father's younger son the language meant
nothing. Along with Howie, he'd stopped taking
Judaism seriously at thirteen—the Sunday after the
Saturday of his bar mitzvah—and had not set foot
since then in a synagogue. He'd even left the space
for religion blank on his hospital admission form,
lest the word "Jewish" prompt a visit to his room by
a rabbi, come to talk in the way rabbis talk. Religion was a lie that he had recognized early in life,
and he found all religions offensive, considered their
superstitious folderol meaningless, childish, couldn't
stand the complete unadultness—the baby talk and
the righteousness and the sheep, the avid believers.
No hocus-pocus about death and God or obsolete
fantasies of heaven for him. There was only our bodies, born to live and die on terms decided by the
bodies that had lived and died before us. If he could

be said to have located a philosophical niche for himself, that was it—he'd come upon it early and intuitively, and however elemental, that was the whole of it. Should he ever write an autobiography, he'd call it *The Life and Death of a Male Body*. But after retiring he tried becoming a painter, not a writer, and so he gave that title to a series of his abstractions.

But none of what he did or didn't believe mattered on the day that his father was buried beside his mother in the rundown cemetery just off the Jersey Turnpike.

Over the gate through which the family entered into the original acreage of the old nineteenth-century cemetery was an arch with the cemetery association's name inscribed in Hebrew; at either end of the arch was carved a six-pointed star. The stone of the gate's two pillars had been badly broken and chipped away—by time and by vandals—and a crooked iron gate with a rusted lock hadn't to be pushed open in order to enter but was half off its hinges and embedded several inches in the ground. Nor had the stone of the obelisk that they passed— inscribed with Hebrew scripture and the names of the family buried at the foot of its plinth—weathered the decades well either. At the head of the crowded rows of upright gravestones stood the old section's one small brick mausoleum, whose filigreed steel door and original two windows—which, at the time of the interment of its occupants, would have been colored with stained glass—had been sealed with concrete blocks to protect against further vandalism, so that now the little square building looked more like an abandoned toolshed or an outdoor toilet no longer in operation than an eternal dwelling place in keeping with the renown, wealth, or status of those who'd constructed it to house their family dead. Slowly they passed between the upright gravestones that were mainly inscribed with Hebrew but that in some cases also bore words in Yiddish, Russian, German, even Hungarian. Most were engraved with the Star of David while others were more elaborately decorated, with a pair of blessing hands or a pitcher or a five-branched candelabrum. At the graves of the young children and infants—and there were more than a handful, though not as many as those of young women who'd died in their twenties, more than likely during childbirth—they came upon an sional gravestone topped with the sculpture of a lamb or decorated with an engraving in the shape of a tree trunk with its upper half sawed away, and as they headed in single file through the crooked, uneven, narrow pathways of the original cemetery toward the newer, parklike northern spaces, where the funeral was to take place, it was possible—in just this little Jewish cemetery, founded in a field on the border of Elizabeth and Newark by, among others, the community-minded father of the late owner of Elizabeth's most beloved jewelry store—to count how many had perished when influenza killed ten million in 1918.

Nineteen eighteen: only one of the terrible years among the plethora of corpse-strewn *anni horribiles* that will blacken the memory of the twentieth century forever.

He stood at the graveside among some two dozen of his relatives, with his daughter at his right, clutching his hand, and his two sons behind him and his wife to the side of his daughter. Merely standing there absorbing the blow that is the death of a father proved to be a surprising challenge to his physical strength—it was a good thing Howie was beside him on the left, one arm holding him firmly around his waist, to prevent anything untoward from happening.

It had never been difficult to know what to make of either his mother or his father. They were a mother and a father. They were imbued with few other desires. But the space taken up by their bodies was now vacant. Their lifelong substantiality was gone. His father's coffin, a plain pine box, was lowered on its straps into the hole that had been dug for him beside his wife's coffin. There the dead man would remain for even more hours than he'd spent selling jewelry, and that was in itself no number to sneer at. He had opened the store in 1933, the year his second son was born, and got rid of it in 1974, having by then sold engagement and wedding rings to three generations of Elizabeth families. How he scrounged up the capital in 1933, how he found *customers* in 1933, was always a mystery to his sons. But it was for them that he had left his job behind the watch counter at Abelson's Irvington store on Springfield Avenue, where he worked nine A.M. to nine P.M. Mondays, Wednesdays, Fridays, and Saturdays, and nine to five on Tuesdays and Thursdays, to open his own little Elizabeth store, fifteen feet wide, with the inscription in black lettering on the display window that read, from day one, "Diamonds—Jewelry—Watches," and in smaller letters beneath, "Fine watch, clock, and jewelry repair." At the age of thirty-two he finally set out to work sixty and seventy hours a week for his family instead of for Moe Abelson's. To lure Elizabeth's big working-class population and to avoid alienating or frightening away the port city's tens of thousands of churchgoing Christians with his Jewish name, he extended credit freely—just made sure they paid at least thirty or forty percent down. He never checked their credit; as long as he got his cost out of it, they could come in afterward and pay a few dollars a week, even nothing, and he really didn't care. He never went broke with credit, and the good will generated by his flexibility was more than worth it. He decorated the shop with a few silver-plated pieces to make it attractive—tea sets, trays, chafing dishes, candlesticks that he sold dirt cheap—and at Christmastime he always had a snow scene with Santa in the window, but the stroke of genius was to call the business not by his name but rather Everyman's Jewelry Store, which was how it was known throughout Union County to the swarms of ordinary people who were his faithful customers until he sold his inventory to the wholesaler and retired at the age of seventy-three. "It's a big deal for working people to buy a diamond," he told his sons, "no matter how small. The wife can wear it for the beauty and she can wear it for the status. And when she does, this guy is not just a plumber—he's a man with a wife with a diamond. His wife owns something that is imperishable. Because beyond the beauty and the status and the value, the diamond is imperishable. A piece of the earth that is imperishable, and a mere mortal is wearing it on her hand!"

The reason for leaving Abelson's, where he'd still been lucky enough to be collecting a paycheck through the crash and into the worst years of the Depression, the reason for daring to open a store of his own in such bad times, was simple: to everyone who asked, and even to those who didn't, he explained, "I had to have something to leave my two boys."

There were two upright shovels with their blades in the large pile of earth to one side of the grave. He had thought they had been left there by the gravediggers, who would use them later to fill the grave. He had imagined that, as at his mother's funeral, each mourner would step up to the hole to throw a clump of dirt onto the coffin's lid, after which they would all depart for their cars. But his father had requested of the rabbi the traditional Jewish rites, and those, he now discovered, called for burial by the mourners and not by employees of the cemetery or anyone else. The rabbi had told Howie beforehand, but Howie, for whatever reason, hadn't told him, and so he was surprised now when his brother, handsomely dressed in a dark suit, a white shirt, a dark tie, and shining black shoes, walked over to pull one of the shovels out of the pile, and then set out to fill the blade until it was brimming with dirt. Then he walked ceremoniously to the head of the grave, stood there a moment to think his thoughts, and, angling the shovel downward a little, let the dirt run slowly out. Upon landing on the wood cover of the coffin, it made the sound that is absorbed into one's being like no other.

Howie returned to plunge the blade of the shovel into the crumbling pyramid of dirt that stood about four feet high. They were going to have to shovel that dirt back into the hole until his father's grave was level with the adjacent cemetery grounds.

It took close to an hour to move the dirt. The elderly among the relatives and friends, unable to wield a shovel, helped by throwing fistfuls of dirt onto the coffin, and he himself could do no more than that, and so it fell to Howie and Howie's four sons and his own two—the six of them all strapping men in their late twenties and early thirties—to do the heavy labor. In teams of two they stood beside the pile and, spadeful by spadeful, moved the dirt from the pile back into the hole. Every few minutes another team took over, and it seemed to him, at one point, as though this task would never end, as though they would be there burying his father forever. The best he could do to be as immersed in the burial's brutal directness as his brother, his sons, and his nephews was to stand at the edge of the grave and watch as the dirt encased the coffin. He watched till it reached the lid, which was decorated only with a carving of the Star of David, and then he watched as it began to cover the lid. His father was going to lie not only in the coffin but under the weight of that dirt, and all at once he saw his father's mouth as if there were no coffin, as if the dirt they were throwing into the grave was being deposited straight down on him, filling up his mouth, blinding his eyes, clogging his nostrils, and closing off his ears. He wanted to tell them to stop, to command them to go no further—he did not want them to cover his father's face and block the passages through which he sucked in life. I've been looking at that face since I was born—stop burying my father's face! But they had found their rhythm, these strong boys, and they couldn't stop and they wouldn't stop, not even if he hurled himself into the grave and demanded that the burial come to a halt. Nothing could stop them now. They would just keep going, burying him, too, if that was necessary to get the job done. Howie was off to the side, his brow covered with sweat, watching the six cousins athletically complete the job, with the goal in sight shoveling at a terrific pace, not like mourners assuming the burden of an archaic ritual but like old-fashioned workmen feeding a furnace with fuel.

Many of the elderly were weeping now and holding on to each other. The pyramid of dirt was gone. The rabbi stepped forward and, after carefully smoothing the surface with his bare hands, used a stick to delineate in the loose soil the dimensions of the grave.

He had watched his father's disappearance from the world inch by inch. He had been forced to follow it right to the end. It was like a second death, one no less awful than the first. Suddenly he was remembering the rush of emotion that carried him down and down into the layers of his life when, at the hospital, his father had picked up each of the three infant grandchildren for the first time, pondering Randy, then later Lonny, then finally Nancy with the same expressive gaze of baffled delight.

"Are you all right?" Nancy asked, putting her arms around him while he stood and looked at the lines the stick had made in the soil, drawn there as if for a children's game. He squeezed her tightly to him and said, "Yes, I'm all right." Then he sighed, even laughed, when he said, "Now I know what it means to be buried. I didn't till today." "I've never seen anything so chilling in my life," Nancy said. "Nor have I," he told her. "It's time to go," he said, and with him and Nancy and Howie in the lead, the mourners slowly departed, though he could not begin to empty himself of all that he'd just seen and thought, the mind circling back even as the feet walked away.

Because a wind had been blowing while the

grave was being filled, he could taste the dirt coat-
ing the inside of his mouth well after they had left
the cemetery and returned to New York.

For the next nine years his health remained stable.
Twice he'd been blindsided by a crisis, but unlike
the boy in the bed next to his, he'd been spared the
disaster. Then in 1998, when his blood pressure began to mount and would not respond to changes
in medication, the doctors determined that he had
an obstruction of his renal artery, which fortunately
had resulted so far in only a minor loss of kid-
ney function, and he entered the hospital for a renal artery angioplasty. Yet again his luck held, and
the problem was resolved with the insertion of a
stent that was transported on a catheter maneu-
vered up through a puncture in the femoral artery
and through the aorta to the occlusion.

He was sixty-five, newly retired, and by now divorced for the third time. He went on Medicare,
began to collect Social Security, and sat down with
his lawyer to write a will. Writing a will—that was
the best part of aging and probably even of dying, the writing and, as time passed, the updating
and revising and carefully reconsidered rewriting of

one's will. A few years later he followed through on the promise he'd made to himself immediately after the 9/11 attacks and moved from Manhattan to the Starfish Beach retirement village at the Jersey Shore, only a couple of miles from the seaside town where his family had vacationed for a portion of every summer. The Starfish Beach condominiums were attractive shingled one-story houses with big windows and sliding glass doors that led to rear outdoor decks; eight units were attached to form a semicircular compound enclosing a shrubbery garden and a small pond. The facilities for the five hundred elderly residents who lived in these compounds, spread over a hundred acres, included tennis courts, a large common garden with a potting shed, a workout center, a postal station, a social center with meeting rooms, a ceramics studio, a woodworking shop, a small library, a computer room with three terminals and a common printer, and a big room for lectures and performances and for the slide shows that were offered by couples who had just returned from their travels abroad. There was a heated Olympic-sized outdoor swimming pool in the heart of the village as well as a smaller indoor pool, and there was a decent restau-

rant in the modest mall at the end of the main village street, along with a bookstore, a liquor store,
a gift shop, a bank, a brokerage office, a realtor, a
lawyer's office, and a gas station. A supermarket was
only a short drive away, and if you were ambulatory,
as most residents were, you could easily walk the
half mile to the boardwalk and down to the wide
ocean beach, where a lifeguard was on duty all summer long.

As soon as he moved into the village, he turned
the sunny living room of his three-room condo into an artist's studio, and now, after taking his daily
hour-long four-mile walk on the boardwalk, he
spent most of the remainder of each day fulfilling
a long-standing ambition by happily painting away,
a routine that yielded all the excitement he'd expected. He missed nothing about New York except
Nancy, the child whose presence had never ceased
to delight him, and who, as a divorced mother of
two four-year-olds, was no longer protected in the
way that he'd hoped. In the aftermath of their daughter's divorce, he and Phoebe—equally weighed down
by anxiety—had stepped in and, separately, spent
more time with Nancy than they had since she'd
gone off to the Midwest to college. There she'd

met the poetic husband-to-be, a graduate student openly disdainful of commercial culture and particularly of her father's line of work, who, once he discovered himself no longer simply half of a quiet, thoughtful couple who liked to listen to chamber music and read books in their spare time but a father of twins, found the tumult of a young family's domestic existence unbearable—especially for someone needing order and silence to complete a first novel—and charged Nancy with fostering this great disaster with her ongoing lament over his impeding her maternal instinct. After work and on weekends he absented himself more and more from the clutter created in their undersized apartment by the needs of the two clamoring tiny creatures he had crazily spawned, and when he finally upped and left his publishing job—and parenthood—he had to go clear back to Minnesota to regain his sanity and resume his thinking and evade as much responsibility as he possibly could.

If her father could have had his way, Nancy and the twins would have moved to the shore too. She could have commuted to work on the Jersey line, leaving the kids with nannies and babysitters costing half as much as help in New York, and he would have been nearby to look after them as well, to take them to and from preschool, to oversee them at the beach, and so on. Father and daughter could have met to have dinner once a week and to take a walk together on weekends. They'd all be living beside the beautiful sea and away from the threat of Al Qaeda. The day after the destruction of the Twin Towers he'd said to Nancy, "I've got a deep-rooted fondness for survival. I'm getting out of here." And just ten weeks later, in late November, he left. The thought of his daughter and her children falling victim to a terrorist attack tormented him during his first months at the shore, though once there he no longer had anxiety for himself and was rid of that sense of pointless risk taking that had dogged him every day since the catastrophe had subverted everyone's sense of security and introduced an in- eradicable precariousness into their daily lives. He was merely doing everything he reasonably could to stay alive. As always—and like most everyone else—he didn't want the end to come a minute ear- lier than it had to.

The year after the insertion of the renal stent, he had surgery for another major obstruction, this one

in his left carotid artery, one of the two main arteries that stretch from the aorta to the base of the
skull and supply blood to the brain and that if left
obstructed could cause a disabling stroke or even
sudden death. The incision was made in the neck,
then the artery feeding the brain was clamped shut
to stop the blood flowing through it. Then it was
slit open and the plaque that was causing the block-
age scraped out and removed. It would have been
a help not to have to face this delicate an operation alone, but Nancy was swamped by her job and
the demands of caring for the children without a
mate, and at that time there was no one else in his
life whom he could ask for assistance. Nor did he
want to disrupt his brother's hectic schedule to tell
him about the surgery and cause him to be concerned, especially as he would be out of the hospital the following morning, providing there were no
complications. This wasn't the peritonitis crisis or
the quintuple bypass surgery—from a medical point
of view it was nothing extraordinary, or so he was
led to believe by the agreeable surgeon, who assured
him that a carotid endarterectomy was a common
vascular surgical procedure and he would be back at
his easel within a day or two.

So he drove off alone in the early morning to the hospital and waited in a glassed-in anteroom on the surgical floor along with another ten or twelve men in hospital gowns scheduled for the first round of operations that day. The room would probably be full like this until as late as four in the afternoon. Most of the patients would come out the other end, and, too, over the course of the weeks, a few might not; nonetheless, they passed the time reading the morning papers, and when the name of one of them was called and he got up to leave for the operating room, he gave his sections of the paper to whoever requested them. You would have thought from the calm in the room that they were going off to get their hair cut, rather than, say, to get the artery leading to the brain sliced open.

At one point, the man to his side, having handed him that day's sports section, quietly began talking to him. He was probably only in his late forties or early fifties, but his skin was pasty and his voice was not strong or assured. "First my mother died," he said, "six months later my father died, eight months after that my only sister died, a year later my marriage broke down and my wife took everything I had. And that's when I began to imagine someone coming to me and saying, 'Now we're going to cut off your right arm as well. Do you think you can take that?' And so they cut off my right arm. Then later they come around and they say, 'Now we're going to cut off your left arm.' Then, when that's done, they come back one day and they say, 'Do you want to quit now? Is that enough? Or should we go ahead and start in on your legs?' And all the time I was thinking, When, when do I quit? When do I turn on the gas and put my head in the oven? When is enough enough? That was how I lived with my grief for ten years. It took ten years. And now the grief is finally over and this shit starts up."

When his turn came, the fellow beside him reached over to take the sports section back, and he was shepherded to the operating room by a nurse. Inside, half a dozen people were moving about in the glare of the lights making preparations for his surgery. He could not locate the surgeon among them. It would have reassured him to see the surgeon's friendly face, but either the doctor hadn't entered the operating room yet or he was off in some corner where he couldn't quite be seen. Several of the younger doctors were already wearing surgical masks, and the look of them made him think of terrorists. One of them asked whether he wanted a general or a local anesthetic, the way a waiter might have asked if he preferred red or white wine. He was confused—why should the decision about anesthesia be made this late? "I don't know. Which is better?" he said. "For us, the local. We can monitor the brain function better if the patient is conscious." "You're telling me that's safer? Is that what you're saying? Then I'll do it."

It was a mistake, a barely endurable mistake, because the operation lasted two hours and his head was claustrophobically draped with a cloth and the cutting and scraping took place so close to his ear, he could hear every move their instruments made as though he were inside an echo chamber. But there was nothing to be done. No fight to put up. You take it and endure it. Just give yourself over to it for as long as it lasts.

He slept well that night, by the next day felt fine, and at noon, after he lied and said a friend was waiting downstairs to pick him up, he was released and went out to the parking lot and cautiously drove himself home. When he got to the condo and sat down in his studio to look at the canvas he could soon resume painting, he burst into tears, just as his father had after he'd got home from his near-fatal bout of peritonitis.

But now, instead of ending, it continued; now not a year went by when he wasn't hospitalized. The son of long-lived parents, the brother of a man six years his senior who was seemingly as fit as he'd been when he'd carried the ball for Thomas Jefferson High, he was still only in his sixties when his health began giving way and his body seemed threatened all the time. He'd married three times, had mistresses and children and an interesting job where he'd been a success, but now eluding death seemed to have become the central business of his life and bodily decay his entire story.

The year after he had carotid artery surgery he had an angiogram in which the doctor discovered that he'd had a silent heart attack on the posterior wall because of an obstructed graft. The news stunned him, though fortunately Nancy had come down by train to accompany him to the hospital and her reassurance helped restore his equanimity. The doctor then went on to perform an angioplasty, and inserted a stent in his left anterior descending artery, after ballooning the artery open where new deposits of plaque had formed. From the table he could watch the catheter being wiggled up into the coronary artery—he was under the lightest sedation and able to follow the whole procedure on the monitor as though his body were somebody else's. A year later he had another angioplasty and another stent installed in one of the grafts, which had begun to narrow. The following year he had to have three stents installed at one go—to repair arterial obstructions whose location, as the doctor told him afterward, made the procedure no picnic to perform.

As always, to keep his mind elsewhere he summoned up his father's store and the names of the nine brands of watches and seven brands of clocks for which his father was an authorized distributor; his father didn't make much money selling watches and clocks, but he loaded up on them because they were a steady item and brought window-shoppers in from the street. What he did with these seed memories during each of his angioplasties was this: he would tune out the badinage the doctors and nurses invariably exchanged while setting up, tune out the rock music pumped into the chilly, sterile room where he lay strapped to the operating table amid all the intimidating machinery designed to keep cardiac patients alive, and from the moment they got to work anesthetizing his groin and puncturing the skin for the insertion of the arterial catheter, he would distract himself by reciting under his breath the lists he'd first alphabetized as a small boy helping at the store after school—"Benrus, Bulova, Croton, Elgin, Hamilton, Helbros, Ovistone, Waltham, Wittnauer"—focusing all the while on the distinctive look of the numerals on the dial of the watch as he intoned its brand name, sweeping from one through twelve and back again. Then he'd start on the clocks—"General Electric, Ingersoll, McClintock, New Haven, Seth Thomas, Telechron, Westclox"—remembering how the wind clocks ticked and the electric clocks hummed until finally he heard the doctor announce that the procedure was over and that everything had gone well. The doctor's assistant, after applying pressure to the wound, placed a sandbag on the groin to prevent bleeding, and with the weight resting there, he had to lie motionless in his hospital bed for the next six hours. His not being able to move was the worst of it, strangely—because of the thousands of involuntary thoughts that suffused the slow-moving time —but the following morning, if all had gone well overnight, he was brought a tray of inedible breakfast to look at and a sheaf of post-angioplasty instructions to follow and by eleven A.M. he would have been discharged. On three separate occasions he'd arrived at home and was hurriedly undressing for a much-needed shower when he'd found a couple of the EKG electrode pads still stuck to him, because the nurse helping to discharge him had forgotten to peel them from his chest and throw them in the garbage. One morning he looked down in the shower to find that no one had bothered to remove the IV feeding needle, a gadget they called a heplock, from his black-and-blue forearm, and so he had to dress and drive over to his internist's office in Spring Lake to have the heplock taken out before it became a source of infection.

The year after the three stents he was briefly knocked out on an operating table while a defibrillator was permanently inserted as a safeguard against the new development that endangered his life and that along with the scarring at the posterior wall of his heart and his borderline ejection fraction made him a candidate for a fatal cardiac arrhythmia. The defibrillator was a thin metal box about the size of a cigarette lighter; it was lodged beneath the skin of his upper chest, a few inches from his left shoulder, with its wire leads attached to his vulnerable heart, ready to administer a shock to correct his heartbeat—and confuse death—if it became perilously irregular.

Nancy had been with him for this procedure too, and afterward, when he got back to his room and he lowered one side of his hospital gown to show her the visible bulge that was the embedded defibrillator, she had to turn away. "Darling," he said to her, "it's to protect me—there's nothing to be upset about." "I know that it's to protect you. I'm glad there is such a thing that's able to protect you. It's just a shock to see because," and finding herself too far along to come up with a comforting lie, she said, "because you've always been so youthful." "Well, I'm more youthful with it than I would be without it. I'll be able to do everything I like to do, only without having to worry about the arrhythmia putting me at serious risk." But she was pale with

helplessness and couldn't stop the tears from running down her face: she wanted her father to be the
way he was when she was ten and eleven and twelve
and thirteen, without impediment or incapacity—
and so did he. She couldn't possibly have wanted it
as much as he did, but for that moment he found
his own sorrow easier to accept than hers. The desire was strong to say something tender to alleviate
her fears, as though, all over again, she were the
more vulnerable of the two.

He never really stopped worrying about her, nor
did he understand how it happened that such a
child should be his. He hadn't necessarily done the
right things to make it happen, even if Phoebe
had. But there are such people, spectacularly good
people—miracles, really—and it was his great fortune that one of these miracles was his own incor-
ruptible daughter. He was amazed when he looked
around himself and saw how bitterly disappointed
parents could be—as he was with his own two sons,
who continued to act as if what had happened to
them had never happened before or since to anyone
else—and then to have a child who was number one
in every way. Sometimes it seemed that everything
was a mistake except Nancy. So he worried about

her, and he still never passed a women's clothing shop without thinking of her and going in to find something she'd like, and he thought, I'm very lucky, and he thought, Some good has to come out somewhere, and it has in her.

He was remembering now her brief period as a track star. When Nancy was thirteen she'd placed second in a race at her all-girls school, a run of about two miles, and she saw the possibility of something in which she could be exceptional. She was good in everything else, but this was another kind of stardom. For a while he gave up swimming at the club first thing so they could run together in the early morning and sometimes, too, in the day's waning hours. They'd go to the park and it would be just the two of them and the shadows and the light. She was running for the school team by then, and during a meet she was rounding a bend when her leg gave way and she fell to the track in agony. What had happened was something that can happen to a girl in early puberty—because the bones don't fully harden by that age, what would have been in a mature woman merely a strained tendon was more dramatic for Nancy: the tendon held but a piece of bone in the hip pulled away. Along with the track coach, he rushed Nancy to the hospital emergency room, where she was in great pain and very fearful, especially when she heard there was nothing to be done, though at the same time she was told, correctly enough, that the injury would heal by itself over a period of time. But that was the end of her track career, not just because recovery would take the rest of the season but because puberty was upon her, and soon her breasts enlarged and her hips widened and the speed that was hers when she had her childish body disappeared. And then, as if the end of her championship running and the alteration of her physique weren't enough to leave her reeling, that very year delivered the misery of her parents' divorce.

When she sat on his hospital bed and wept in his arms it was for many reasons, not least for his having left her when she was thirteen. She'd come to the shore to assist him and all his cool-headed and sensible daughter could do was relive the difficulties that had resulted from the divorce and confess to the undying fantasy of a parental reconciliation that she had spent more than half of her life hoping for. "But there's no remaking reality," he said softly, rubbing her back and stroking her hair and rocking her gently in his arms. "Just take it as it comes. Hold your ground and take it as it comes. There's no other way."

That was the truth and the best he could do— and exactly what he'd told her many years earlier, when he held her in his arms in the taxi coming home from the emergency room while she shook with sobs because of the inexplicable turn of events.

All these procedures and hospitalizations had made him a decidedly lonelier, less confident man than he'd been during the first year of retirement. Even his cherished peace and quiet seemed to have been turned into a self-generated form of solitary confinement, and he was hounded by the sense that he was headed for the end. But instead of moving back to attackable Manhattan, he decided to oppose the sense of estrangement brought on by his bodily failings and to enter more vigorously into the world around him. He did this by organizing two weekly painting classes for the village residents, an after-noon class for beginners and an evening class for those already somewhat familiar with paints.

There were about ten students in each class, and they loved meeting in his bright studio room. By and large, learning to paint was a pretext for their being there, and most of them were taking the class for the same reason he was giving it: to find satisfying contact with other people. All but two were older than he, and though they assembled each week in a mood of comradely good cheer, the conversation invariably turned to matters of sickness and health, their personal biographies having by this time become identical with their medical biographies and the swapping of medical data crowding out nearly everything else. At his studio, they more readily identified one another by their ailments than by their painting. "How is your sugar?" "How is your pressure?" "What did the doctor say?" "Did you hear about my neighbor? It spread to the liver." One of the men came to class with his portable oxygen unit. Another had Parkinson's tremors but was eager to learn to paint anyway. All of them without exception complained—sometimes jokingly, sometimes not—about increasing memory loss, and they spoke of how rapidly the months and the seasons and the years went by, how life no longer moved at the same speed. A couple of the women were being treated for cancer. One had to leave halfway through the course to return to the hospital for treatment. Another woman had a bad back and occasionally had to lie on the floor at the edge of the room for ten or fifteen minutes before she could get up and resume working in front of her easel. After the first few times, he told her she should go into his bedroom instead and lie down for as long as she liked on his bed—it had a firm mattress and she would be more comfortable. Once when she did not come out of the bedroom for half an hour, he knocked and, when he heard her crying inside, opened the door and went in.

She was a lean, tall, gray-haired woman, within a year or two of his age, whose appearance and gentleness reminded him of Phoebe. Her name was Millicent Kramer, and she was the best of his students by far and, coincidentally, the least messy. She alone, in what he charitably called "Advanced Painting," managed to finish each class without having dripped paint all over her running shoes. He never heard her say, as others did, "I can't get the paint to do what I want it to do," or "I can picture it in my mind but I can't seem to get it on the canvas," nor did he ever have to tell her, "Don't be intimidated, don't hold back." He tried to be generous to them all, even the hopeless ones, usually those very ones who came in and said right off, "I had a great day —I feel inspired today." When finally he'd heard enough of that, he repeated to them something he vaguely remembered Chuck Close's having said in an interview: amateurs look for inspiration; the rest of us just get up and go to work. He didn't start them with drawing, because barely a one of them was able to draw, and a figure would have set up all sorts of problems of proportion and scale, so instead, after they'd finished a couple of sessions going over the rudiments (how to lay their paints out and arrange their palettes, and so on) and familiarizing themselves with the medium itself, he set up a still life on a table—a vase, some flowers, a piece of fruit, a teacup—and encouraged them to use it as a reference point. He told them to be creative in order to try to get them to loosen up and use their whole arm and paint, if possible, without fear. He told them they didn't have to worry about what the arrangement actually looked like: "Interpret it," he told them, "this is a creative act." Unfortunately, saying that sometimes led to his having to tell someone, "You know, maybe you shouldn't make the vase six times larger than the teacup." "But you told me I should interpret it" was invariably the reply, to which, as kindly as he could, he in turn replied, "I didn't want that much interpretation." The art-class misery he least wished to deal with was their painting from imagination; yet because they were very enthusiastic about "creativity" and the idea of letting yourself go, those remained the common themes from one session to the next. Sometimes the worst occurred and a student said, "I don't want to do flowers or fruit, I want to do abstraction like you do." Since he knew there was no way to discuss what a beginner is doing when he does what he calls an abstraction, he told the student, "Fine—why don't you just do whatever you like," and when he walked around the studio, dutifully giving tips, he would find, as expected, that after looking at an attempt at an abstract painting, he had nothing to say except "Keep working." He tried to link painting to play rather than to art by quoting Picasso to them, something along the lines of their having to regain the child in order to paint like a grownup. Mainly what he did was to replicate what he'd heard as a kid when he started taking classes and his teachers were telling him the same things.

He was only called upon to be at all specific

when he stood beside Millicent and saw what she could do and how fast she got better. He could sense right off that she had a knack that was innate and that far exceeded what little gift some of the others began to demonstrate as the weeks went by. It was never a question with her of combining the red and the blue right off the palette but rather of modifying the mixture with a little black or with just a bit of the blue so that the colors were interestingly harmonious, and her paintings had coherence instead of falling apart everywhere, which was what he confronted much of the time when he went from easel to easel and, for lack of anything else he could think of, heard himself saying, "That's coming along well." Millicent did need to be reminded "Don't overwork it," but otherwise nothing he suggested was wasted on her and she would look for the slightest shade of meaning in whatever he told her. Her way of painting seemed to arise directly from her instincts, and if her painting didn't look like anyone else's in the class, it wasn't solely because of stylistic distinction but because of the way she felt and perceived things. Others varied in their neediness; though the class was largely full of good will, some still resented it when they needed help at all, and even inadvertent criticism could make one of the men, a former CEO of a manufacturing company, frighteningly touchy. But never Millicent: she would have been the teacher's most rewarding pupil in anyone's amateur painting class.

Now he sat beside her on the bed and took her hand in his, thinking: When you are young, it's the outside of the body that matters, how you look externally. When you get older, it's what's inside that matters, and people stop caring how you look.

"Don't you have some medication you can take?" he asked her.

"I took it," she said. "I can't take any more. It doesn't help but for a few hours anyway. Nothing helps. I've had three operations. Each one is more extensive than the last and more harrowing than the last, and each one makes the pain worse. I'm sorry I'm in such a state. I apologize for this."

Near her head on the bed was a back brace she'd removed in order to lie down. It consisted of a white plastic shell that fit across the lower spine and attached to a web of elasticized cloth and Velcro straps that fastened snugly over the stomach an oblong piece of felt-lined canvas. Though she remained in her white painting smock, she had removed the brace and tried to push it out of sight under a pillow when he opened the door and walked in, which was why it was up by her head and impossible not to be continually mindful of while they talked. It was only a standard back brace, worn under the outer clothing, whose plastic posterior section was no more than eight or nine inches high, and yet it spoke to him of the perpetual nearness in their affluent retirement village of illness and death.

"Would you like a glass of water?" he asked her.

He could see by looking into her eyes how difficult the pain was to bear. "Yes," she said weakly, "yes, please."

Her husband, Gerald Kramer, had been the owner, publisher, and editor of a county weekly, the leading local paper, that did not shy away from exposing corruption in municipal government up and down the shore. He remembered Kramer, who'd grown up a slum kid in nearby Neptune, as a compact, bald, opinionated man who walked with considerable swagger, played aggressive, ungainly tennis, owned a little Cessna, and ran a discussion group once a week on current events—the most popular evening event on the Starfish Beach calendar along with the screenings of old movies sponsored by the film society—until he was felled by brain cancer and was to be seen being pushed around the village streets in a wheelchair by his wife. Even in retirement he'd continued to have the air of an omnipotent being dedicated all his life to an important mission, but in those eleven months before he died he seemed pierced by bewilderment, dazed by his diminishment, dazed by his helplessness, dazed to think that the dying man enfeebled in a wheelchair—a man no longer able to smash a tennis ball, to sail a boat, to fly a plane, let alone to edit a page of the *Monmouth County Bugle*—could answer to his name. One of his dashing eccentricities was, for no special reason, to dress up from time to time in his tuxedo to partake of the veal scaloppine at the village restaurant with his wife of fifty-odd years. "Where the hell else am I going to wear it?" was the gruffly engaging explanation that went out to one and all—he could sometimes woo people with an unexpected charm. After the surgery, however, his wife had to sit beside him and wait for him to crookedly open his mouth and then feed him gingerly, the swaggering husband, the roughneck gallant, with a spoon. Many people knew Kramer and admired him and out on the street wanted to say hello and ask after his health, but often his wife had to shake her head to warn them away when he was in the depths of his despondency—the vitriolic despondency of one once assertively in the middle of everything who was now in the middle of nothing. Was himself now nothing, nothing but a motionless cipher angrily awaiting the blessing of an eradication that was absolute.

"You can continue to lie here if you like," he said to Millicent Kramer after she had drunk some of the water.

"I can't be lying down all the time!" she cried. "I just cannot do it anymore! I was so agile, I was so active—if you were Gerald's wife, you had to be. We went everywhere. I felt so free. We went to China, we went all over Africa. Now I can't even take the bus to New York unless I'm laced to the gills with painkillers. And I'm not good with the painkillers—they make me completely crazy. And by the time I get there I'm in pain anyway. Oh, I'm sorry about this. I'm terribly sorry. Everybody here has their ordeal. There's nothing special about my story and I'm sorry to burden you with it. You probably have a story of your own."

"Would a heating pad help?" he asked.

"You know what would help?" she said. "The sound of that voice that's disappeared. The sound of the exceptional man I loved. I think I could take all this if he were here. But I can't without him. I never saw him weaken once in his life—then came the cancer and it crushed him. I'm not Gerald. He would just marshal all his forces and do it—marshal all his everything and do whatever it was that had to be done. But I can't. I can't take the pain anymore. It overrides everything. I think sometimes that I can't go on another hour. I tell myself to ignore it. I tell myself it doesn't matter. I tell myself, 'Don't engage it. It's a specter. It's an annoyance, it's nothing more than that. Don't accord it power. Don't cooperate with it. Don't take the bait. Don't respond. Muscle through. Barrel through. Either you're in charge or it's in charge—the choice is yours!' I repeat this to myself a million times a day, as though I'm Gerald speaking, and then suddenly it's so awful I have to lie down on the floor in the middle of the supermarket and all the words are meaningless. Oh, I'm sorry, truly. I abhor tears."

"We all do," he told her, "but we cry anyway."

"This class has meant so much to me," she said. "I spend the whole week waiting for it. I'm like a schoolkid about this class," she confessed, and he found her looking at him with a childish trust, as though she were indeed a little one being put to sleep—and he, like Gerald, could right anything.

"Do you have any of your medication with you?" he asked.

"I already took one this morning."

"Take another," he told her.

"I have to be so careful with those pills."

"I understand. But do yourself a favor and take another now. One more can't do much harm, and it'll get you over the hump. It'll get you back to the easel."

"It takes an hour for it to work. The class will be over."

"You're welcome to stay and keep painting after the others go. Where is the medication?"

"In my purse. In the studio. By my easel. The old brown bag with the worn shoulder strap."

He brought it to her, and with what was left of the water in the glass, she took the pill, an opiate that killed pain for three or four hours, a large, white lozenge-shaped pill that caused her to relax with the anticipation of relief the instant she swallowed it. For the first time since she'd begun the class he could see unmistakably how attractive she must have been before the degeneration of an aging spine took charge of her life.

"Lie here until it starts to work," he said. "Then come join the class."

"I do apologize for all this," she said as he was leaving. "It's just that pain makes you so alone." And here the fortitude gave way again and left her sobbing into her hands. "It's so shameful."

"There's nothing shameful about it."

"There is, there is," she wept. "The not being able to look after oneself, the pathetic need to be comforted . . ."

"In the circumstances, none of that is remotely shameful."

"You're wrong. You don't know. The dependence, the helplessness, the isolation, the dread—it's all so ghastly and shameful. The pain makes you frightened of yourself. The utter otherness of it is awful."

She's embarrassed by what she's become, he thought, embarrassed, humiliated, humbled almost beyond her own recognition. But which of them wasn't? They were all embarrassed by what they'd become. Wasn't he? By the physical changes. By the diminishment of virility. By the errors that had contorted him and the blows—both those self-inflicted and those from without—that deformed him. What lent a horrible grandeur to the process of reduction suffered by Millicent Kramer—and miniaturized by comparison the bleakness of his own—was, of course, the intractable pain. Even those pictures of the grandchildren, he thought, those photographs that grandparents have all over the house, she probably doesn't even look at anymore. Nothing anymore but the pain.

"Shhh," he said, "shhh, quiet down," and he returned to the bed to momentarily take her hand again before heading back to the class. "You wait for the painkiller to work and come back in when you're ready to paint."

Ten days later she killed herself with an overdose of sleeping pills.

At the end of the twelve-week session virtually everyone wanted to sign up for a second one, but he announced that a change of plans would make it impossible for him to resume giving the courses until the following fall.

*   *   *

When he'd fled New York, he'd chosen the shore as his new home because he'd always loved swimming in the surf and battling the waves, and because of the happy childhood associations he had with this stretch of Jersey beach, and because, even if Nancy wouldn't join him, he'd be just over an hour away from her, and because living in a relaxing, comfortable environment was bound to be beneficial to his health. There was no woman in his life other than his daughter. She never failed to call before leaving for work each morning, but otherwise his phone seldom rang. The affection of the sons of his first marriage he no longer pursued; he had never done the right thing by their mother or by them, and to resist the repetitiveness of these accusations and his sons' version of family history would require a measure of combativeness that had vanished from his arsenal. The combativeness had been replaced by a huge sadness. If he yielded in the solitude of his long evenings to the temptation to call one or the other of them, he always felt saddened afterward, saddened and beaten.

Randy and Lonny were the source of his deepest

guilt, but he could not continue to explain his behavior to them. He had tried often enough when they were young men—but then they were too young and angry to understand, now they were too old and angry to understand. And what was there to understand? It was inexplicable to him—the excitement they could seriously persist in deriving from his denunciation. He had done what he did the way that he did it as they did what they did the way they did it. Was their steadfast posture of unforgivingness any more forgivable? Or any less harmful in its effect? He was one of the millions of American men who were party to a divorce that broke up a family. But did he beat their mother? Did he beat them? Did he fail to support their mother or fail to support them? Did any one of them ever have to beg money from him? Was he ever once severe? Had he not made every overture toward them that he could? What could have been avoided? What could he have done differently that would have made him more acceptable to them other than what he could not do, which was to remain married and live with their mother? Either they understood that or they didn't—and sadly for him (and for them), they didn't. Nor could they ever understand that he had lost the same family they did. And no doubt there were things he still failed to understand. If so, that was no less sad. No one could say there wasn't enough sadness to go around or enough remorse to prompt the fugue of questions with which he attempted to defend the story of his life.

He told them nothing about his string of hospitalizations for fear that it might inspire too much vindictive satisfaction. He was sure that when he died they would rejoice, and all because of those earliest recollections they'd never outgrown of his leaving his first family to start a second. That he had eventually betrayed his second family for a beauty twenty-six years his junior who, according to Randy and Lonny, anyone other than their father could have spotted as a "nutcase" a mile away —a model, no less, "a brainless model" he'd met when she was hired by his agency for a job that carried the entire crew, including the two of them, to the Caribbean for a few days' work—had only reinforced their view of him as an underhanded, irresponsible, frivolously immature sexual adventurer. As a father, he was an impostor. As a husband, even to the incomparable Phoebe, for whom he jettisoned their mother, he was an impostor. As anything but a cunthound, he was a fake through and through. And as for his becoming an "artist" in his old age, that, to his sons, was the biggest joke of all. Once he took up painting in earnest every day, the derisive nickname coined by Randy for their father was "the happy cobbler."

In response he did not claim either moral rectitude or perfect judgment. His third marriage had been founded on boundless desire for a woman he had no business with but a desire that never lost its power to blind him and lead him, at fifty, to play a young man's game. He had not slept with Phoebe for the previous six years, yet he could not offer this intimate fact of their life as an explanation to his sons for his second divorce. He didn't think that his record as Phoebe's husband for fifteen years, as Nancy's live-in father for thirteen years, as Howie's brother and his parents' son since birth, required him to make such an explanation. He did not think that his record as an advertising man for over twenty years required him to make such an explanation. He did not think that his record as father to *Lonny* and *Randy* required such an explanation!

Yet their description of how he'd conducted himself over a lifetime was not even a caricature but, in his estimation, a portrayal of what he was not, a description with which they persisted in minimizing everything worthwhile that he believed was apparent to most everyone else. Minimized his decency, then magnified his defects, for a reason that surely could not continue to carry such great force at this late date. Into their forties they remained with their father the children that they'd been back when he'd first left their mother, children who by their nature could not understand that there might be more than one explanation to human behavior—children, however, with the appearance and aggression of men, and against whose undermining he could never manage to sustain a solid defense. They elected to make the absent father suffer, and so he did, investing them with that power. Suffering his wrongdoing was all he could ever do to please them, to pay his bill, to indulge like the best of dads their maddening opposition.

You wicked bastards! You sulky fuckers! You condemning little shits! Would everything be different, he asked himself, if I'd been different and done things differently? Would it all be less lonely than it is now? Of course it would! But this is what I did! I am seventy-one. This is the man I have made. This is what I did to get here, and there's nothing more to be said!

Over the years, luckily, he heard regularly from Howie. In his late fifties Howie, like almost all the partners who reached that age except for the top three or four, had retired from Goldman Sachs; by then he was worth easily fifty million dollars. He was soon sitting on numerous corporate boards, eventually being named chairman of Procter & Gamble, for whom he'd done arbitrage in his early days. In his seventies, still vigorous and eager to be working, he'd become a consultant to a Boston buyout firm specializing in financial institutions and traveled to look for potential acquisitions. Yet despite the continuing responsibilities and the demands on Howie's time, the two brothers exchanged phone calls a couple of times a month, calls that could sometimes go on for as long as half an hour, with one of them laughingly entertaining the other with recollections of their years growing up and of comical moments from their days at school and in the jewelry store.

Now, though, when they spoke, an unwarranted coldness came over him, and to his brother's jo-

viality his response was silence. The reason was ridiculous. He hated Howie because of his robust
good health. He hated Howie because he'd never
in his life been a patient in a hospital, because dis-
ease was unknown to him, because nowhere was
his body scarred from the surgical knife, nor were
there six metal stents lodged in his arteries along
with a cardiac alarm system tucked into the wall of
his chest that was called a defibrillator, a word that
when he first heard it pronounced by his cardiologist was unknown to him and sounded, innocuously
enough, as if it had something to do with the gear
system of a bicycle. He hated him because, though
they were offspring of the same two parents and
looked so very much alike, Howie had inherited the
physical impregnability and he the coronary and
vascular weaknesses. It was ridiculous to hate him,
because there was nothing Howie could do about
his good health other than to enjoy it. It was ridiculous to hate Howie for nothing other than having
been born himself and not someone else. He'd never
envied him for his athletic or academic prowess, for
his financial wizardry and his wealth, never envied
him even when he thought of his own sons and
wives and then of Howie's—four grown boys who

continued to love him and the devoted wife of fifty years who clearly was as important to him as he to her. He was proud of the muscular, athletic brother who rarely got less than an A in school, and had admired him since earliest childhood. Himself a youngster with an artistic talent whose single noteworthy physical skill was swimming, he'd loved Howie unabashedly and followed him everywhere. But now he hated him and he envied him and he was poisonously jealous of him and, in his thoughts, all but rose up in rage against him because the force that Howie brought to bear on life had in no way been impeded. Though on the phone he suppressed as best he could everything irrational and indefensible that he felt, as the months passed their calls took up less time and became less frequent, and soon they were hardly speaking at all.

He did not retain for long the spiteful desire for his brother to lose his health—that far he could not go as an envier, since his brother's losing his health would not result in his regaining his own. Nothing could restore his health, his youth, or invigorate his talent. He could, nonetheless, in a frenzied mood, almost reach a point where he could believe that Howie's good health was responsible for his own compromised health, even though he knew better, even though he was not without a civilized person's tolerant understanding of the puzzle of inequality and misfortune. Back when the psychoanalyst had glibly diagnosed the symptoms of severe appendicitis as a case of envy, he was still very much his parents' son and barely acquainted with the feelings that come with believing that the possessions of another might better belong to you. But now he knew; in his old age he had discovered the emotional state that robs the envier of his serenity and, worse, his realism—he hated Howie for that biological endowment that should have been his as well.

Suddenly he could not stand his brother in the primitive, instinctual way that his sons could not stand him.

He had been hoping there would be a woman in the painting classes in whom he might take an interest—that was half the reason for giving them. But pairing up with one of the widows his age toward whom he felt no attraction proved to be beyond him, though the robustly healthy young women he saw jogging along the boardwalk when he took his morning walk, still all curves and gleaming hair and, to his eyes, seemingly more beautiful than their counterparts of an earlier era had ever been, were not sufficiently lacking in common sense to exchange with him anything other than a professionally innocent smile. Following their speedy progress with his gaze was a pleasure, but a difficult pleasure, and at bottom the mental caress was a source of biting sadness that only intensified an unbearable loneliness. True, he had chosen to live alone, but not unbearably alone. The worst of being unbearably alone was that you had to bear it—either that or you were sunk. You had to work hard to prevent your mind from sabotaging you by its looking hungrily back at the superabundant past.

And he'd become bored with his painting. For many years he'd dreamed of the uninterrupted span of time that his retirement would afford him to paint—as had thousands and thousands of other art directors who'd also earned their livelihood working in ad agencies. But after painting almost every day since moving to the shore, he had run out of interest in what he was doing. The urgent demand to paint had lifted, the enterprise designed to fill the rest of his life fizzled out. He had no more ideas. Every picture he worked on came out looking like the last one. His brightly colored abstractions had always been prominently displayed in the Starfish Beach show of local artists, and of the three that were taken by a gallery in the nearby seaside tourist town, all had been sold to the gallery's best customers. But that was nearly two years ago. Now he had nothing to show. It had all come to nothing. As a painter he was and probably always had been no more than the "happy cobbler" he happened to know he'd been dubbed by the satirical son. It was as though painting had been an exorcism. But designed to expel what malignancy? The oldest of his self-delusions? Or had he run to painting to attempt to deliver himself from the knowledge that you are born to live and you die instead? Suddenly he was lost in nothing, in the sound of the two syllables "nothing" no less than in the nothingness, lost and drifting, and the dread began to seep in. Nothing comes without risk, he thought, nothing, nothing—there's nothing that doesn't backfire, not even painting stupid pictures!

He explained to Nancy, when she asked about his work, that he'd had "an irreversible aesthetic vasectomy."

"Something will start you again," she said, accepting the hyperbolic language with an absolving laugh. She had been permeated by the quality of her mother's kindness, by the inability to remain aloof from another's need, by the day-to-day earthborn soulfulness that he had disastrously undervalued and thrown away—thrown away without beginning to realize all he would subsequently live without.

"I don't think it will," he was saying to their daughter. "There's a reason I was never a painter. I've run smack up against it."

"The reason you weren't a painter," Nancy explained, "is because you've had wives and children. You had mouths to feed. You had responsibilities."

"The reason I wasn't a painter was because I'm not a painter. Not then and not now."

"Oh, Dad—"

"No, listen to me. All I've been doing is doodling away the time."

"You're just upset right now. Don't insult yourself—it's not so. I know it's not so. I have your paintings all over my apartment. I look at them every day, and I can promise you I'm not looking at doodlings. People come over—they look at them.

They ask me who the artist is. They pay attention to them. They ask if the artist is living."

"What do you tell them?"

"Listen to *me* now: they're not responding to doodlings. They're responding to work. To work that is beautiful. And of course," she said, and now with that laugh that left him feeling washed clean and, in his seventies, infatuated with his girl-child all over again, "of course I tell them you're living. I tell them my father painted these, and I'm so proud to say that."

"Good, sweetie."

"I've got a little gallery going here."

"That's good—that makes me feel good."

"You're just frustrated now. It's just that simple. You're a wonderful painter. I know what I'm talking about. If there's anybody in this world equipped to know if you're a wonderful painter or not, it's me."

After all he'd put her through by betraying Phoebe, she still wanted to praise him. From the age of ten she'd been like that—a pure and sensible girl, besmirched only by her unstinting generosity, harmlessly hiding from unhappiness by blotting out the faults of everyone dear to her and by overloving love. Baling forgiveness as though it were so much hay. The harm inevitably came when she concealed from herself just a little too much that was wanting in the makeup of the ostentatiously brilliant young crybaby she had fallen for and married.

"And it's not just me, Dad. It's everybody who comes. I was interviewing babysitters the other day, because Molly can't do it anymore. I was interviewing for a new babysitter and this wonderful girl I ended up hiring, Tanya—she's a student looking to earn some extra money, she's at the Art Students League just like you were—she couldn't take her eyes off the one I have in the dining room, over the sideboard, the yellow one—you know the one I mean?"

"Yes."

"She couldn't take her eyes off it. The yellow and black one. It was really quite something. I was asking her these questions and she was focused over the sideboard. She asked when it was painted and where I had bought it. There's something very compelling about your work."

"You're very sweet to me, darling."

"No. I'm candid with you, that's all."

"Thank you."

"You'll get back to it. It'll happen again. Painting isn't through with you yet. Just enjoy yourself in the meantime. It's so beautiful where you are. Just be patient. Just take your time. Nothing's vanished. Enjoy the weather, enjoy your walks, enjoy the beach and the ocean. Nothing's vanished and nothing's altered."

Strange—all the comfort he was taking from her words and yet he wasn't convinced for a second that she knew what she was talking about. But the wish to take comfort, he realized, is no small thing, particularly from the one who miraculously still loves you.

"I don't go in the surf anymore," he told her.

"You don't?"

It was only Nancy, but he felt humiliated nonetheless by the confession. "I've lost the confidence for the surf."

"You can swim in the pool, can't you?"

"I can."

"Okay, so swim in the pool."

He asked her then about the twins, thinking if only he were still with Phoebe, if only Phoebe were with him now, if only Nancy hadn't to work so hard to shore him up in the absence of a devoted wife, if only he hadn't wounded Phoebe the way that he had, if only he hadn't wronged her, if only he hadn't lied! If only she hadn't said, "I can never trust you to be truthful again."

It didn't begin until he was nearly fifty. The young women were everywhere—photographers' reps, secretaries, stylists, models, account executives. Lots of women, and you worked and traveled and had lunch together, and what was astonishing wasn't what happened—the acquisition by a husband of "someone else"—but that it took so long to happen, even after the passion had dwindled and disappeared from his marriage. It began with a pretty, dark-haired young woman of nineteen whom he hired to work as his secretary and who, within two weeks of taking the job, was kneeling on his office floor with her ass raised and him fucking her fully clothed, with just his fly unzipped. He had not possessed her by coercion, though he had indeed taken her by surprise—but then he, who was conscious of having no peculiarities to flaunt and who believed himself content to live by the customary norms, to behave more or less the same as others, had taken himself no less by surprise. It was an easy entry because she was so moist and, in those daredevil circumstances, it took no time for each of them to achieve a vigorous orgasm. One morning just after she had gotten up from the floor and returned to her desk in the outer office, and while he was still standing, face flushed, in the middle of the room and adjusting his clothing, his boss, Clarence, the group management supervisor and an executive vice president, opened the door and came in. "Where is her apartment?" Clarence asked him. "I don't know," he replied. "Use her apartment," Clarence said severely and left. But they couldn't stop what they were doing where and how they were doing it, even though theirs was one of those office trapeze acts in which everyone has everything to lose. They were too close to each other all day to stop. All either of them could think about was her kneeling on his office floor and him hurling her skirt up over her back and grabbing her by the hair and, after pushing aside her underpants, penetrating her as forcefully as he could and with an utter disregard for discovery.

Then came the shoot in Grenada. He was running the show, and he and the photographer he hired picked the models, ten of them for a towel ad that would be set beside a small natural pool in the tropical forest, with each model clad in a short summer robe, her head turbaned in the client's towel as though she'd just washed her hair. The arrangements had been made, the ad okayed, and he was on the plane sitting alone away from everyone else so he could read a book and fall asleep and fly there unperturbed.

They had a stop in the Caribbean, and he got off the plane and went into the waiting room and looked around, saw all the models, and said hello to them before everyone got onto another, smaller plane and took a short hop to their destination, where they were picked up by several cars and by a small jeeplike vehicle, which he decided to ride in with one of the models whom he'd taken note of when she was hired. She was the only foreign model on the shoot, a Dane named Merete and probably, at twenty-four, the oldest of the ten; the rest were American girls, eighteen and nineteen years old. There was somebody driving, Merete was in the middle, and he was on the outside. It was nighttime and very dark. They were squeezed in tightly together and he had his arm around the top of her seat. Only moments after the car took off his thumb was in her mouth, and without his knowing it, his marriage had come under assault. The young man who started out hoping never to live two lives was about to cleave himself open with a hatchet.

When they got to the hotel and he went to his room, he lay there most of the night thinking only of Merete. The next day when they met, she said to him, "I waited for you." The whole thing was so quick and so intense. They shot all day in the middle of the forest with the small natural pool, worked hard and seriously for the entire day, and when they got back he found that the photographer's rep who was along on the job had rented a house on the beach just for him—he had thrown a lot of work her way, and so the rep rented it for him and he moved out of the hotel and Merete came with him and they lived there on the beach together for three days. In the early morning when he was coming back up the beach from his swim, she would be waiting on the veranda wearing just her bikini underpants. They would start then and there, while he was still wet from his long swim. For the first two days he was always diddling around her ass with his fingers while she went down on him, until finally she looked up and said, "If you like that little hole, why don't you use it?"

Of course he saw her back in New York. Every day that she was free he would go to her place at lunchtime. Then one Saturday he, Phoebe, and Nancy were walking down Third Avenue when he saw Merete walking on the other side of the street with that easy, upright, somnambulant gait whose feral assuredness always slayed him, as if she were not approaching the Seventy-second Street light carrying a bag of groceries but serenely traversing the Serengeti, Merete Jespersen of Copenhagen grazing the grasses of the savanna amid a thousand African antelope. Models didn't all have to be needle-thin in those days, and even before he spotted her by her glide and saw the sheaf of golden hair down her back, he identified her as his very own treasure, the white hunter's prize, by the weight of her breasts inside her blouse and the light heft of the behind whose little hole had come to afford them such delight. He displayed neither fear nor excitement upon seeing her, though he felt extremely ill and had to get to a phone alone to call her—getting to the phone was all he thought about for the rest of the afternoon. This wasn't ravishing the secretary on the office floor. This was the raw supremacy of her creatureliness over his instinct for survival, itself a force to be reckoned with. This was the wildest venture of his life, the one, as he was only faintly beginning to understand, that could wipe out everything. Only in passing did it occur to him that it might be somewhat delusional at the age of fifty to think that he could find a hole that would substitute for everything else.

A few months later he flew to Paris to see her. She had been working in Europe for six weeks, and though they spoke secretly on the phone as often as three times a day, that wasn't sufficient to satisfy the longing in either of them. A week before the Saturday when he and Phoebe were to drive to New Hampshire to bring Nancy home from summer camp, he told Phoebe that he would have to fly to Paris for a shoot that weekend. He'd leave on Thursday night and be home by Monday morning. Ezra Pollock, the account executive, would be going with him and they would meet up with a European crew over there. He knew that Ez was with his family until after Labor Day, unreachable on a tiny phoneless island several miles out to sea from South Freeport, Maine, so far from everything that seals could be seen socializing on the ledges of the rocky island nearby. He gave Phoebe the name and

number of the Paris hotel and then reconsidered
ten times a day his risking the chance of being discovered by her just so he and Merete could spend
a long weekend together in the lovers' capital of
the world. But Phoebe remained unsuspicious and
seemed to be looking forward to picking up Nancy
by herself. She was eager to have her home after a
summer away, just as he was dying to see Merete after a month and a half apart, and so he flew off on
Thursday night, his mind on that little hole and
what she liked him to do with it. Yes, fixed dream-
ily on no more than that all the way across the Atlantic on Air France.

What went wrong was the weather. High winds
and blustery storms swept through Europe, and
no planes were able to take off all day Sunday and
into Monday. Both days he sat at the airport with
Merete, who had come along to cling to him until
the last possible moment, but when it was clear that
there would be no departures from de Gaulle until
Tuesday at the earliest, they took a taxi back to the
Rue des Beaux Arts, to Merete's favorite swank little Left Bank hotel, where they were able to rebook
their room, the room mirrored with smoked glass.
During every night ride they took by taxi in Paris,

they performed the same impudent playlet, always as though inadvertently and for the first time: he'd drop his hand onto her knee and she'd let her legs fall open just far enough so that he could reach up under her silk slip of a dress—nothing more, really, than a piece of deluxe lingerie—and finger her while she adjusted her head to look idly out of the taxi at the illuminated shop windows and he, leaning back in his seat, pretended to be anything but riveted by the way she could continue to behave as if no one were touching her even as he sensed her beginning to come. Merete carried everything erotic to the limit. (Earlier, in a discreet antique jewelry shop down the street from their hotel, he'd adorned her throat with a stunning trinket, a pendant necklace set with diamonds and demantoid garnets and strung on its original gold chain. Like the knowledgeable son of his father that he was, he'd asked to examine the stones through the jeweler's loupe. "What are you looking for?" Merete asked. "Flaws, cracks, the coloring—if nothing appears under a ten-power magnification the diamond can be certified as flawless. You see? My father's words issue from my mouth whenever I speak about jewelry." "But not about anything else," she said. "Not about anything about you. Those words are mine." Not while shopping, not while walking the streets, not while taking an elevator or having coffee together in a booth around the corner from her apartment, could they ever stop seducing each other. "How do you know how to do that, to hold the thing—?" "The loupe." "How do you know how to hold the loupe in your eye like that?" "My father taught me. You just tighten your socket around it. Rather like you do." "So what color is it?" "Blue. Blue-white. That was the best in the old days. My father would say it still is. My father would say, 'Beyond the beauty and the status and the value, the diamond is imperishable.' 'Imperishable' was a word he loved to savor." "Who doesn't?" Merete said. "What is it in Danish?" he asked her. "'*Uforgængelig.*' It's just as wonderful." "Why don't we take it?" he told the saleswoman, who in turn, speaking in perfect English and with a touch of French—and with perfect cunning—told the young companion of the older gentleman, "Mademoiselle is very lucky. *Une femme choyée,*" and the cost was about as much as the entire inventory of the Elizabeth store, if not more, back when he was running one-hundred-dollar engagement rings of a quarter or a half carat to be sized for his father's

customers by a man working on a bench in a cubbyhole on Frelinghuysen Avenue circa 1942.) And now
he withdrew the finger sticky with her slime, per-
fumed her lips with it, then pressed it between her
teeth for her tongue to caress, reminding her of their
first meeting and what they'd dared to do as strang-
ers, an American adman of fifty and a Danish model
of twenty-four, crossing a Caribbean island in the
dark, transfixed. Reminding her that she was his and
he hers. A cult of two.

There was a message from Phoebe waiting for him
at the hotel: "Contact me immediately. Your mother
gravely ill."

When he phoned he learned that his eighty-
year-old mother had had a stroke at five A.M. Monday, New York time, and was not expected to live.

He explained to Phoebe about the weather con-
ditions and learned that Howie was already on his
way east and that his father was keeping vigil beside
his mother's bed. He wrote down the telephone
number of his mother's room at the hospital, and
Phoebe told him that as soon as she hung up, she
would be heading over to Jersey herself, to be with
his father at the hospital until Howie arrived. She

had only been waiting for him to call her back. "I missed you by a few minutes this morning. The desk clerk told me, 'Madame and monsieur have just departed for the airport.'"

"Yes," he said, "I shared a cab with the photographer's rep."

"No, you shared a cab with the Danish twenty-four-year-old with whom you are having an affair. I'm sorry, but I can no longer look the other way. I looked the other way with that secretary. But the humiliation has now gone too far. Paris," she said with disgust. "The planning. The premeditation. The tickets and the travel agent. Tell me, which of you romantic cornballs dreamed up Paris for your sneaky little undertaking? Where did you two eat? What charming restaurants did you go to?"

"Phoebe, I don't know what you're talking about. You're not making any sense. I'll get the first plane back that I possibly can."

His mother died an hour before he was able to reach the hospital in Elizabeth. His father and his brother were sitting beside the body that lay beneath the covers of the bed. He had never before seen his mother in a hospital bed, though of course she had seen him there more than once. Like Howie, she had enjoyed perfect health all her life. It was she who would rush to the hospital to comfort others. Howie said, "We haven't told the staff she died. We waited. We wanted you to be able to see her before they took her away." What he saw was the high-relief contour of an elderly woman asleep. What he saw was a stone, the heavy, sepulchral, stonelike weight that says, Death is just death—it's nothing more.

He hugged his father, who patted his hand and said, "It's best this way. You wouldn't have wanted her to live the way that thing left her."

When he took his mother's hand and held it to his lips, he realized that in a matter of hours he had lost the two women whose devotion had been the underpinning of his strength.

With Phoebe he lied and lied and lied, but to no avail. He told her that he had gone to Paris to break off the affair with Merete. He'd had to see her face to face to do it, and that's where she was working.

"But in the hotel, while you were breaking off the affair, didn't you sleep with her at night in the same bed?"

"We didn't sleep. She cried all night long."

"For four whole nights? That's a lot of crying for

a twenty-four-year-old Dane. I don't think even Hamlet cried that much."

"Phoebe, I went to tell her it was over—and it *is* over."

"What did I do so wrong," Phoebe asked, "that you should want to humiliate me like this? Why should you want to unhinge *everything?* Has it all been so hideous? I should get over being dumbstruck, but I can't. I, who never doubted you, to whom it rarely occurred even to question you, and now I can never believe another word you say. I can never trust you to be truthful again. Yes, you wounded me with the secretary, but I kept my mouth shut. You didn't even know I knew, did you? Well, did you?"

"I didn't, no."

"Because I hid my thoughts from you—unfortunately I couldn't hide them from myself. And now you wound me with the Dane and you humiliate me with the lying, and now I will *not* hide my thoughts and keep my mouth shut. A mature, intelligent woman comes along, a mate who understands what reciprocity is. She rids you of Cecilia, gives you a phenomenal daughter, changes your entire life, and you don't know what to do for her except to fuck the Dane. Every time I looked at my watch I kept figuring what time it was in Paris and what you two would be doing. That went on for the whole weekend. The basis of everything is trust, is it not? Is it not?"

She had only to say Cecilia's name to instantaneously recall the vindictive tirades visited on his mother and father by his first wife, who, fifteen years later, to his horror, turned out to have been not merely abandoned Cecilia but his Cassandra: "I pity this little Miss Muffet coming after me— I genuinely do pity the vile little Quaker slut!"

"You can weather anything," Phoebe was telling him, "even if the trust is violated, if it's owned up to. Then you become life partners in a different way, but it's still possible to remain partners. But lying—lying is cheap, contemptible control over the other person. It's watching the other person acting on incomplete information—in other words, humiliating herself. Lying is so commonplace and yet, if you're on the receiving end, it's such an astonishing thing. The people you liars are betraying put up with a growing list of insults until you really can't help but think less of them, can you? I'm sure that liars as skillful and persistent and devious as you reach the point where it's the one you're lying to, and not you, who seems like the one with the serious limitations. You probably don't even think you're lying—you think of it as an act of kindness to spare the feelings of your poor sexless mate. You probably think your lying is in the nature of a virtue, an act of generosity toward the dumb cluck who loves you. Or maybe it's just what it is—a fucking lie, one fucking lie after another. Oh, why go on—all these episodes are so well known," she said. "The man loses the passion for the marriage and he cannot live without. The wife is pragmatic. The wife is realistic. Yes, passion is gone, she's older and not what she was, but to her it's enough to have the physical affection, just being there with him in the bed, she holding him, he holding her. The physical affection, the tenderness, the comradery, the closeness . . . But he cannot accept that. Because he is a man who *cannot live without.* Well, you're going to live without now, mister. You're going to live without plenty. You're going to find out what living without is all about! Oh, go away from me, please. I can't bear the role you've reduced me to. The pitiful middle-aged wife, embittered by rejection, consumed by rotten jealousy! Raging! Repugnant! Oh,

I hate you for that more than anything. Go away, leave this house. I can't bear the sight of you with that satyr-on-his-good-behavior look on your face! You'll get no absolution from me—never! I will not be trifled with any longer! Go, please! Leave me alone!"

"Phoebe—"

"No! Don't you dare call me by my name!"

But these episodes are indeed well known and require no further elaboration. Phoebe threw him out the night after his mother's burial, they were divorced after negotiating a financial settlement, and because he did not know what else to do to make sense of what had happened or how else to appear responsible—and to rehabilitate himself particularly in Nancy's eyes—a few months later he married Merete. Since he had broken everything up because of this person half his age, it seemed only logical to go ahead and tidy everything up again by making her his third wife—never was he clever enough as a married man to fall into adultery or to fall in love with a woman who was not free.

It was not long afterward that he discovered that Merete was something more than that little hole, or perhaps something less. He discovered her inability to think anything through without all her uncertainties intruding and skewing her thought. He discovered the true dimensions of her vanity and, though she was only in her twenties, her morbid fear of aging. He discovered her green card problems and her long-standing tax mess with the IRS, the result of years of failing to file a return. And when he required emergency coronary artery surgery, he discovered her terror of illness and her uselessness in the face of danger. Altogether he was a little late in learning that all her boldness was encompassed in her eroticism and that her carrying everything erotic between them to the limit was their only overpowering affinity. He had replaced the most helpful wife imaginable with a wife who went to pieces under the slightest pressure. But in the immediate aftermath, marrying her had seemed the simplest way to cover up the crime.

Passing the time was excruciating without painting. There was the hour-long morning walk, in the late afternoon there was twenty minutes of working out with his light weights and a half hour of doing easy laps at the pool—the daily regime his cardiologist encouraged—but that was it, those were the events of his day. How much time could you spend staring out at the ocean, even if it was the ocean you'd loved since you were a boy? How long could he watch the tides flood in and flow out without his remembering, as anyone might in a sea-gazing reverie, that life had been given to him, as to all, randomly, fortuitously, and but once, and for no known or knowable reason? On the evenings he drove over to eat broiled bluefish on the back deck of the fish store that perched at the edge of the in-let where the boats sailed out to the ocean under the old drawbridge, he sometimes stopped first at the town where his family had vacationed in the summertime. He got out of the car on the ocean road and went up onto the boardwalk and sat on one of the benches that looked out to the beach and the sea, the stupendous sea that had been changing continuously without ever changing since he'd been a bony sea-battling boy. This was the very bench where his parents and grandparents used to sit in the evenings to catch the breeze and enjoy the boardwalk promenade of neighbors and friends, and this was the very beach where his family had picnicked and sunned themselves and where he and Howie and their pals went swimming, though it

was now easily twice as wide as it had been then because of a reclamation project recently engineered
by the army. Yet wide as it was, it was still his beach
and at the center of the circles in which his mind
revolved when he remembered the best of boyhood. But how much time could a man spend remembering the best of boyhood? What about enjoying the best of old age? Or was the best of old
age just that—the longing for the best of boyhood,
for the tubular sprout that was then his body and
that rode the waves from way out where they began
to build, rode them with his arms pointed like an
arrowhead and the skinny rest of him following behind like the arrow's shaft, rode them all the way in
to where his rib cage scraped against the tiny sharp
pebbles and jagged clamshells and pulverized sea-
shells at the edge of the shore and he hustled to his
feet and hurriedly turned and went lurching through
the low surf until it was knee high and deep enough
for him to plunge in and begin swimming madly
out to the rising breakers—into the advancing, green
Atlantic, rolling unstoppably toward him like the
obstinate fact of the future—and, if he was lucky,
make it there in time to catch the next big wave and
then the next and the next and the next until from

the low slant of inland sunlight glittering across the water he knew it was time to go. He ran home barefoot and wet and salty, remembering the mightiness of that immense sea boiling in his own two ears and licking his forearm to taste his skin fresh from the ocean and baked by the sun. Along with the ecstasy of a whole day of being battered silly by the sea, the taste and the smell intoxicated him so that he was driven to the brink of biting down with his teeth to tear out a chunk of himself and savor his fleshly existence.

Quickly as he could on his heels he crossed the concrete sidewalks still hot from the day and when he reached their rooming house headed around back to the outdoor shower with the soggy plywood walls, where wet sand plopped out of his suit when he kicked it off over his feet and held it up to the cold water beating down on his head. The level force of the surging tide, the ordeal of the burning pavement, the bristling shock of the ice-cold shower, the blessing of the taut new muscles and the slender limbs and the darkly suntanned flesh marked by just a single pale scar from the hernia surgery hidden down by his groin—there was nothing about those August days, after the German submarines had been destroyed and there were no more drowned sailors to worry about, that wasn't wonderfully clear. And nothing about his physical perfection that he had any reason not to take for granted.

When he returned from dinner he would try to settle in and read. He had a library of oversized art books filling one wall of the studio; he had been accumulating and studying them all his life, but now he couldn't sit in his reading chair and turn the pages of a single one of them without feeling ridiculous. The delusion—as he now thought of it—had lost its power over him, and so the books only magnified his sense of the hopelessly laughable amateur he was and of the hollowness of the pursuit to which he had dedicated his retirement.

Trying to pass more than a little time in the company of the Starfish Beach residents was also unendurable. Unlike him, many were able not merely to construct whole conversations that revolved around their grandchildren but to find sufficient grounds for existence in the existence of their grandchildren. Caught in their company, he sometimes experienced loneliness in what felt like its purest form. And even those among the village residents who

were thoughtful, well-spoken people were not interesting to be with more than once in a while.
Most of the elderly residents had been settled into
their marriages for decades and were sufficiently
connected still to whatever was left of their marital
felicity that only rarely could he get the husband to
go off by himself for lunch without the wife. However wistfully he might sometimes look at such couples as dusk approached or on Sunday afternoons,
there were the rest of the hours of the week to
think about, and theirs wasn't a life for him when
he was on top of his melancholy. The upshot was
that he should never have moved into such a com-
munity in the first place. He had displaced himself
just when what age most demanded was that he be
rooted as he'd been for all those years he ran the
creative department at the agency. Always he had
been invigorated by stability, never by stasis. And
this was stagnation. There was an absence now of
all forms of solace, a barrenness under the heading
of consolation, and no way to return to what was. A
sense of otherness had overtaken him—"otherness,"
a word in his own language to describe a state of
being all but foreign to him till his art student Millicent Kramer had jarringly used it to bemoan her

condition. Nothing any longer kindled his curiosity or answered his needs, not his painting, not his family, not his neighbors, nothing except the young women who jogged by him on the boardwalk in the morning. My God, he thought, the man I once was! The life that surrounded me! The force that was mine! No "otherness" to be felt anywhere! Once upon a time I was a full human being.

There was one particular girl whom he never failed to wave to when she jogged by, and one morning he set out to meet her. Always she waved back and smiled, and then forlornly he watched her run on. This time he stopped her. He called out, "Miss, miss, I want to talk to you," and instead of shaking her head no and breezing by with a "Can't now," as he fully imagined her doing, she turned and jogged back to where he was waiting, by the plank stairs that led down to the beach, and stood with her hands on her hips only a foot away from him, damp with perspiration, a tiny creature perfectly formed. Until she fully relaxed, she pawed the boardwalk with one running shoe like a pony while looking up at this unknown man in the sunglasses who was six feet three and had a full head of wavy gray hair. It

turned out, fortuitously, that she had been working for seven years at an ad agency in Philadelphia,
lived here at the shore, and was currently on her
two-week vacation. When he told her the name of
the New York agency where he'd worked for nearly
a lifetime she was terrifically impressed; his em-
ployer was legendary, and for the next ten minutes
they made the kind of advertising talk that had
never interested him. She would have to be in her
late twenties and yet, with her long, crinkly auburn
hair tied back and in her running shorts and tank
top, and small as she was, she might have been taken
for fourteen. He tried repeatedly to prevent his
gaze from falling to the swell of the breasts that
rose and fell with her breathing. This was torment
to walk away from. The idea was an affront to common sense and a menace to his sanity. His excitement was disproportionate to anything that had
happened or that possibly could happen. He had
not just to hide his hunger; so as not to go mad he
had to annihilate it. Yet he doggedly continued on
as he had planned, still half believing that there was
some combination of words that would somehow
save him from defeat. He said, "I've noticed you
jogging." She surprised him by responding, "I've

noticed you noticing me." "How game are you?" he heard himself asking her, but feeling that the encounter was now out of his control and that everything was going much too fast—feeling, if it were possible, even more reckless than when he'd draped that pendant necklace costing a small fortune around Merete's neck in Paris. Phoebe the devoted wife and Nancy the cherished child were home in New York, awaiting his return—he'd spoken to Nancy the day before, within only hours of her getting back from summer camp—and still he'd told the saleswoman, "We'll take it. You needn't wrap it. Here, Merete, let me do it. I teethed on these clasps. It's called a tubular box clasp. In the thirties, it would have been the safest one around for a piece like this. Come, give me your throat." "What do you have in mind?" the jogger boldly replied, so boldly that he felt at a disadvantage and did not know how forthright to make his answer. Her belly was tanned and her arms were thin and her prominent buttocks were round and firm and her slender legs were strongly muscled and her breasts were substantial for someone not much more than five feet tall. She had the curvaceous lusciousness of a Varga Girl in the old 1940s magazine illustrations, but a miniaturized, childlike Varga Girl, which was why he had begun waving to her in the first place.

He'd said, "How game are you?" and she'd replied, "What do you have in mind?" Now what? He removed his sunglasses so she could see his eyes when he stared down at her. Did she understand what she was implying by answering him like that? Or was it something she said just to be saying something, just to be sounding in charge of herself even as she was feeling frightened and out of her depth? Thirty years ago he wouldn't have doubted the result of pursuing her, young as she was, and the possibility of humiliating rejection would never have occurred to him. But lost was the pleasure of the confidence, and with it the engrossing playfulness of the exchange. He did his best to conceal his anxiety—and the urge to touch—and the craving for just one such body—and the futility of it all—and his insignificance—and apparently succeeded, for when he took a piece of paper from his wallet and wrote down his phone number, she didn't make a face and run off laughing at him but took it with an agreeable little catlike smile that could easily have been accompanied by a purr. "You know where I am," he said, feeling himself growing hard in his pants unbelievably, magically quickly, as though he were fifteen. And feeling, too, that sharp sense of individualization, of sublime singularity, that marks a fresh sexual encounter or love affair and that is the opposite of the deadening depersonalization of serious illness. She scanned his face with two large, lively blue eyes. "There's something in you that's unusual," she said thoughtfully. "Yes, there is," he said and laughed, "I was born in 1933." "You look pretty fit to me," she told him. "And you look pretty fit to me," he replied. "You know where to find me," he said. Engagingly she swung the piece of paper in the air as though it were a tiny bell and to his delight shoved it deep into her damp tank top before taking off down the boardwalk again.

She never called. And when he took his walks he never saw her again. She must have decided to do her jogging along another stretch of the boardwalk, thereby thwarting his longing for the last great outburst of everything.

Shortly after the folly with the childlike Varga Girl in the running shorts and the tank top, he decided to sell the condominium and move back to New York. He considered his giving up on the shore a failure, almost as painful a failure as what had happened to him as a painter in the past half year. Even before 9/11 he had contemplated a retirement of the kind he'd been living for three years now; the disaster of 9/11 had appeared to accelerate his opportunity to make a big change, when in fact it had marked the beginning of his vulnerability and the origin of his exile. But now he'd sell the condo and try to find a place in New York close to Nancy's apartment on the Upper West Side. Because the condo's value had almost doubled in the short time he'd owned it, he might be able to shell out enough cash down to buy a place up by Columbia big enough for all of them to live together under one roof. He'd pay the household expenses and she could meet her own expenses with the child support. She could cut back to working three days a week and spend four full days with the children, as she'd been wanting to do—but couldn't afford to do—since she'd returned to her job from maternity leave. Nancy, the twins, and himself. It was a plan worth proposing to her. She might not mind his assistance, and he was hungering for the company of an intimate to whom he could give and from whom he could receive, and who better in all the world than Nancy?

He allowed himself a couple of weeks to deter-
mine how workable the plan was and to gauge how
desperate he might seem presenting it. Finally, when
he'd decided that for the time being he would pro-
pose nothing to Nancy but rather go into New
York for a day to begin on his own to investigate
the possibility of finding an apartment in his price
range that could comfortably accommodate the
four of them, the rush of bad news came over the
phone, first about Phoebe and the next day about
three of his former colleagues.

He learned of Phoebe's stroke when the phone
rang a little after six-thirty in the morning. It was
Nancy calling from the hospital. Phoebe had phoned
her about an hour earlier to tell her that something
was happening to her, and by the time Nancy got
her to the emergency room her speech was so thick
she could barely make herself understood and she'd
lost movement in her right arm. They had just finished the MRI and Phoebe was now resting in her
room.

"But a stroke, someone as youthful and healthy
as your mother? Was it something to do with the
migraines? Is that possible?"

"They think it was from the medication she was

taking for the migraines," Nancy said. "It was the first drug that had ever helped. She realized the medication posed a minute danger of causing a stroke. She knew that. But once she found that it worked, once she was rid of that pain for the first time in fifty years, she decided it was worth the risk. She'd had three miraculous years pain free. It was bliss."

"Till now," he said sadly. "Till this. Do you want me to drive up?"

"I'll let you know. Let's see how things go. They believe she's out of trouble."

"Will she recover? Will she be able to speak?"

"The doctor says so. He thinks she'll recover one hundred percent."

"Wonderful," he said, but thought, Let's see what he thinks a year from now.

Without his even asking her, Nancy told him, "When she leaves the hospital, she's going to come to stay with me. Matilda will be there during the day and I'll be there the rest of the time." Matilda was the Antiguan nanny who'd begun looking after the children once Nancy had gone back to work.

"That's good," he said.

"It's going to be a total recovery, but the rehab will take a long time."

He was to have driven into New York that very day to begin the search for an apartment for all of them; instead, after consulting Nancy, he went into the city to visit Phoebe at the hospital and then drove back to the shore that evening to resume his life there alone. Nancy, the twins, and himself—it had been a ridiculous idea to begin with, and unfair as well, an abdication of the pledge he'd made to himself after having moved to the shore, which was to insulate his all too responsive daughter from the fears and vulnerabilities of an aging man. Now that Phoebe was so ill, the change he'd imagined for them was impossible anyway, and he determined never to entertain any such plan for Nancy again. He could not let her see him as he was.

At the hospital, Phoebe lay there looking stunned. In addition to the slurred speech caused by the stroke, her voice was barely audible, and she was having difficulty swallowing. He had to sit right up against the hospital bed in order to understand what she was saying. They hadn't been this close to each other's limbs in over two decades, not since he'd gone off to Paris and was there with Merete when his own mother had the stroke that killed her.

"Paralysis is terrifying," she told him, staring down

at the lifeless right arm by her side. He nodded.
"You look at it," she said, "you tell it to move . . ."
He waited while the tears rolled down her face
and she struggled to finish the sentence. When she
couldn't, he finished it for her. "And it doesn't," he
said softly. Now she nodded, and he remembered
the heated eruption of fluency that had come in the
wake of his betrayal. How he wished she could
scald him in that lava now. Anything, anything, an
indictment, a protest, a poem, an ad campaign for
American Airlines, a one-page ad for the *Reader's
Digest*—anything as long as she could recover her
speech! Playfully-full-of-words Phoebe, frank and
open Phoebe, muzzled! "It's everything you can
imagine," she painstakingly told him.

Her beauty, frail to begin with, was smashed and
broken, and tall as she was, under the hospital sheets
she looked shrunken and already on the way to
decomposing. How could the doctor dare to tell
Nancy that the mercilessness of what had befallen
her mother would leave no enduring mark? He
leaned forward to touch her hair, her soft white
hair, doing his best not to cry himself and remembering again—the migraines, Nancy's birth, the day
he'd come upon Phoebe Lambert at the agency,

fresh, frightened, intriguingly innocent, a properly raised girl and, unlike Cecilia, unclouded by a crushing history of childhood chaos, everything about her sound and sane, blessedly not prone to outbursts, and yet without her being at all simple: the very best in the way of naturalness that Quaker Pennsylvania and Swarthmore College could produce. He remembered her reciting from memory for him, unostentatiously and in flawless Middle English, the prologue to *The Canterbury Tales* and, too, the surprising antique locutions she'd picked up from her starchy father, things like "We must be at pains to understand this" and "It is not going too far to say," which could have made him fall for her even without that first glimpse of her striding single-mindedly by his open office door, a mature young woman, the only one in the office who wore no lipstick, tall and bosomless, her fair hair pulled back to reveal the length of her neck and the delicate small-lobed ears of a child. "Why do you laugh sometimes at what I say," she asked him the second time he took her to dinner, "why do you laugh when I'm being perfectly serious?" "Because you charm me so, and you're so unaware of your charm." "There's so much to learn," she said while he ac-

companied her home in the taxi; when he replied
softly, without a trace of the urgency he felt, "I'll
teach you," she had to cover her face with her hands.
"I'm blushing. I blush," she said. "Who doesn't?"
he told her, and he believed that she'd blushed because she thought he was referring not to the sub-
ject of their conversation—all the art she'd never
seen—but to sexual ardor, as indeed he was. He
wasn't thinking in the taxi of showing her the Rem-
brandts at the Metropolitan Museum but of her long
fingers and her wide mouth, though soon enough
he'd take her not just to the Metropolitan but to
the Modern, the Frick, and the Guggenheim. He
remembered her removing her bathing suit out of
sight in the dunes. He remembered them, later in
the afternoon, swimming back together across the
bay. He remembered how everything about this candid, unaffected woman was so unpredictably excit-
ing. He remembered the nobility of her straightness.
Against her own grain, she sparkled. He recalled
telling her, "I can't live without you," and Phoebe's
replying, "Nobody has ever said that to me before," and his admitting, "I've never said it before
myself."

The summer of 1967. She was twenty-six.

Then the next day came news of the former colleagues, the same men he worked with and often ate lunch alongside while they were all with the agency. One was a creative supervisor named Brad Karr, who'd been hospitalized for suicidal depression; the second was Ezra Pollock, who had terminal cancer at seventy; and the third, his boss, was a gentle, lucid bigwig who walked around with the company's most profitable accounts in his pocket, who was almost maternal toward his favorites, who had been suffering for years with heart trouble and the aftereffects of a stroke, and whose picture he was stunned to see in the obituary section of the *Times:* "Clarence Spraco, Wartime Eisenhower Aide and Advertising Innovator, Dies at 84."

He immediately called Clarence's wife at their retirement home up in the Berkshires.

"Hello, Gwen," he said.

"Hi, dear. How are you?"

"I'm okay. How are you doing?" he asked.

"I'm doing all right. My kids came. I have a lot of company. And a lot of help. There are so many things I could tell you. In a sense, I was prepared, and in a way one never is. When I came home I found him dead on the floor, and that was a terrible shock. He had been dead for a couple of hours at that point. He seemed to have died at lunchtime. I had gone out for lunch, and so forth. You know, for him it was a good end. It was sudden, and he didn't have another stroke that would have debilitated him and put him in the hospital."

"Was it a stroke or was it a heart attack?" he asked her.

"It was a myocardial infarct."

"Had he been feeling ill?"

"Well, his blood pressure had been—well, he had a lot of trouble with his blood pressure. And then this past weekend he wasn't feeling so great. His blood pressure had gone up again."

"They couldn't control that with drugs?"

"They did. He took all kinds of drugs. But he probably had a lot of arterial damage. You know, bad old arteries, and there's a point at which the body wears out. And he was so weary at that point. He said to me just a couple of nights ago, 'I'm so weary.' He wanted to live, but there wasn't anything anybody could do to keep him alive any longer. Old age is a battle, dear, if not with this, then with that. It's an unrelenting battle, and just when you're at your weakest and least able to call up your old fight."

"That was a very nice tribute to him in the obituary today. They recognized that he was someone special. I wish I'd had a chance to tell them a few things about his wonderful ability to recognize the value of the people who worked with him. I saw his picture today," he said, "and I remembered a day years ago when a client had taken me to lunch at the Four Seasons, and we were heading down those stairs into the lobby there, and we bumped into Clarence. And my client was feeling expansive and he said, 'Clarence, how are you? Do you know this young art director?' And Clarence said, 'I do. Thank God I do. Thank God the agency does.' He did this again and again, and not just with me."

"He had the highest regard for you, dear. He meant every word of that. I remember," she said, "how he plucked you out of the bullpen when you weren't at the agency even a year. He came home and told me about you. Clarence had an eye for creative talent, and he plucked you out of the bullpen and made you into an art director before you'd even completed your penal servitude working on brochures."

"He was good to me. I always thought of him as the general."

"He'd only been a colonel under Eisenhower."

"He was a general to me. I could tell you dozens of things that are in my mind now." Clarence's suggestion that he fuck his secretary in her apartment rather than in his office wasn't among them.

"Please do. When you talk about him, it's as if he's still here," Gwen said.

"Well, there was the time when we worked and worked every night for two or three weeks until after midnight, sometimes until two or three in the morning, for the Mercedes-Benz pitch. This was really one of the big ones, and we worked like hell, and we didn't get it. But when it was over Clarence said to me, 'I want you and your wife to go to London for a long weekend. I want you to stay at the Savoy because it's my favorite hotel, and I want you and Phoebe to have dinner at the Connaught. And it's on me.' In those days, this was a huge gift, and he gave it even though we'd lost the account. I wish I could have told that to the papers, and all the stories like it."

"Well, the press has been superb," Gwen said. "Even up here. There was an article about him in today's *Berkshire Eagle*. It was long, with a wonderful picture, and very laudatory. They made much of what he'd done in the war and about his being the army's youngest full colonel. I think Clarence would have been amused and contented by the recognition he's gotten."

"Look, you sound, for the moment, okay."

"Well, of course, it's okay now—I'm busy and I've got lots of company. The hard part is going to be when I'm alone."

"What are you going to do? Are you going to stay on in Massachusetts?"

"Yes, I am, for now. I discussed it with Clarence. I said, 'If I'm the one who's left, I'm going to sell the house and go back to New York.' But the kids want me not to do that, because they think I ought to give myself a year."

"Probably they're right. People regret, sometimes, the actions they take right off."

"I think so," she said. "And how is Nancy?"

"She's fine."

"Whenever I think of Nancy as a child, a smile comes to my face. She was pure life. I remember the two of you singing 'Smile' together at our house. We were living in Turtle Bay. It was an afternoon so long ago. You'd taught it to her. She must have been all of six. 'Smile, tho' your heart is aching'—how does it go?—'smile even tho' it's breaking—' You bought her the Nat 'King' Cole record. Remember? I do."

"I do too."

"Does she? Does Nancy?"

"I'm sure she does. Gwen, my heart and thoughts are with you."

"Thank you, dear. So many people have called. The phone has been going steadily for two days. So many people have wept, so many people have told me what he meant to them. If Clarence could only see all this. He knew his value to the company, but you know he also needed the same reassurances that everyone needs in this world."

"Well, he was awfully important to all of us. Look, we'll talk more," he said.

"Okay, dear. I so appreciate your calling."

It took him a while to go back to the phone with a voice he could trust. Brad Karr's wife told him the Manhattan hospital where Brad was a psychiatric patient. He was able to dial Brad's room directly, remembering as he did the time they'd done that slice-of-life commercial for Maxwell House coffee, when they were kids in their twenties, just starting out together, teamed up as a copywriter and an art director, and they broke the bank on the day-after recall score. They got a 34, the highest score in the history of Maxwell House. It was the day of the group Christmas party, and Brad, knowing Clarence would be coming, had his sidekick make cardboard buttons saying "34," and everybody wore them, and Clarence stopped by just to congratulate Brad and him and even put on a button, and they were on their way.

"Hello, Brad? Your old buddy calling from the Jersey Shore."

"Hi. Hello there."

"What's up, kid? I called your house a few minutes ago. I just had a yen to talk to you after all this time, and Mary told me you were in the hospital. That's how I've reached you. How are you doing?"

"Well, I'm doing all right. As such things go."

"How are you feeling?"

"Well, there are better places to be."

"Is it awful?"

"It could be worse. I mean, this happens to be a

pretty good one. It's okay. I don't recommend it for a holiday, but it's been all right."

"How long have you been there?"

"Oh, about a week." Mary Karr had just told him that it had been a month at this point, and that it was his second stay in a year, and that things hadn't been so great in between. Brad's speech was very slow and faltering—probably from the medication —and heavy with hopelessness. "I expect I'll be out soon," he said.

"What do you do all day?"

"Oh, you cut out paper dolls. Things like that. I wander up and down the hallways. Try to keep my sanity."

"What else?"

"Take therapy. Take drugs. I feel like I'm a depository for every drug you can name."

"In addition to the antidepressant, there's other stuff?"

"Yeah. It's mostly a downer. It's not the tranquilizers, it's the antidepressants. They're working, I think."

"Are you able to sleep?"

"Oh yeah. At first there was a little problem, but now they've gotten that part straightened out."

"Do you talk to a doctor during the day?"

"Yeah." Brad laughed, and for the first time sounded something like himself. "He doesn't do any good. He's nice. He tells you to buck up and everything's going to be all right."

"Bradford, remember when you were pissed at Clarence about something and gave him two weeks' notice? I told you not to leave. You said, 'But I've resigned.' 'Rescind your resignation,' I said. And you did. Who else but Clarence and what other agency would have put up with that crap from a copywriter? You did it twice, as I remember. And stayed another ten years."

He'd gotten Brad to laugh again. "Yeah, I was always nuts," Brad said.

"We worked together for a lot of years. Endless silent hours together, hundreds and hundreds, maybe thousands and thousands of silent hours together in your office or mine trying to figure things out."

"That was something," Brad said.

"You bet it was. *You* were something. And don't forget it."

"Thanks, buddy."

"And so what about leaving?" he asked Brad. "When do you think that's going to happen?"

"Well, I don't really know. I imagine it's a matter of a couple of weeks. Since I've been here I've been far less depressed than when I was out. I feel almost composed. I think I'm going to recover."

"That's good news. I'll call you again. I hope to speak to you under better circumstances very shortly."

"Okay. Thanks for calling," Brad said. "Thanks a lot. I'm awfully glad you called."

After hanging up, he wondered: Did he know it was me? Did he truly remember what I remembered? From the voice alone I can't imagine he'll ever get out of there.

Then the third call. He couldn't stop himself from making it, though learning of Brad's hospitalization and Clarence's death and seeing the damage caused by Phoebe's stroke had given him enough to ponder for a while. As did Gwen's reminding him of his teaching Nancy to sing "Smile" like Nat "King" Cole. This call was to Ezra Pollock, who wasn't expected to live out the month but who, astonishingly, when he answered the phone, sounded like someone happy and fulfilled and no less cocky than usual.

"Ez," he said, "what's cookin'? You sound elated."

"I rise to conversation because conversation is my only recreation."

"And you're not depressed?"

"Not at all. I don't have time to be depressed. I'm all concentration." Laughing, Ezra said, "I see through everything now."

"Yourself included?"

"Yes, believe it or not. I've stripped away my bullshit and I'm getting down to brass tacks at last. I've begun my memoir of the advertising business. Before you go, you've got to face the facts, Ace. If I live, I'll write some good stuff."

"Well, don't forget to include how you'd walk into my office and say, 'Okay, here's your panic deadline—first thing tomorrow I need that storyboard in my hand.'"

"It worked, didn't it?"

"You were diligent, Ez. I asked you one time why that fucking detergent *was* so gentle to a lady's delicate hands. You gave me twenty pages on aloes. I got the art director's award for that campaign, and it was because of those pages. It should have been yours. When you get better we'll have lunch and I'll bring you the statue."

"That's a deal," Ez said.

"And how's the pain? Is there pain?"

"Yes, there is, I have it. But I've learned how to handle it. I've got special medicines and I've got five doctors. Five. An oncologist, a urologist, an internist, a hospice nurse, and a hypnotist to help me overcome the nausea."

"The nausea from what, from therapy?"

"Yeah, and the cancer gives you nausea too. I throw up liberally."

"Is that the worst of it?"

"Sometimes my prostate feels like I'm trying to excrete it."

"Can't they take it out?"

"It wouldn't do any good. It's too late for that. And it's a big operation. My weight is down. My blood is down. It would make me so weak and I'd have to give up the treatment, too. It's a big lie that it moves slowly," Ezra said. "It moves like lightning. I didn't have anything in my prostate in the middle of June, but by the middle of August it had spread too far to cut it out. It really moves. So look to your prostate, my boy."

"I'm sorry to hear all this. But I'm glad to hear that you sound as you do. You're yourself, only more so."

"All I want is to write this memoir," Ez said. "I've talked about it long enough, now I have to write it. All that happened to me in that business. If I can write this memoir, I will have told people who I am. If I can write that, I'll die with a grin on my face. How about you, are you working happily? Are you painting? You always said you would. Are you?"

"Yes, I do it. I do it every day. It's fine," he lied.

"Well, I could never write this book, you know. Once I retired I immediately had blocks. But as soon as I got cancer most of my blocks fell away. I can do whatever I want now."

"That's a brutal therapy for writer's block."

"Yeah," Ez said, "I think it is. I don't advise it. You know, I may make it. Then we'll have that lunch and you'll give me the statue. If I make it, the doctors say I can have a normal life."

If he already had a hospice nurse, it seemed unlikely that the doctors would have said such a thing. Though maybe they had to lift his spirits, or maybe he'd imagined they had, or maybe it was just arrogance speaking, that wonderful, ineradicable arrogance of his. "Well, I'm rooting for you, Ez," he said. "If you should want to speak to me, here's my number." He gave it to him.

"Good," Ezra said.

"I'm here all the time. If you feel in the mood, do it, call me. Anytime. Will you?"

"Great. I will."

"All right. Very good. Bye."

"Bye. Bye for now," Ezra said. "Polish up the statue."

For hours after the three consecutive calls—and after the predictable banality and futility of the pep talk, after the attempt to revive the old esprit by reviving memories of his colleagues' lives, by trying to find things to say to buck up the hopeless and bring them back from the brink—what he wanted to do was not only to phone and speak to his daughter, whom he found in the hospital with Phoebe, but to revive his own esprit by phoning and talking to his mother and father. Yet what he'd learned was nothing when measured against the inevitable onslaught that is the end of life. Had he been aware of the mortal suffering of every man and woman he happened to have known during all his years of professional life, of each one's painful story of regret and loss and stoicism, of fear and panic and isolation and dread, had he learned of every last thing they had parted with that had once been vitally theirs

and of how, systematically, they were being destroyed, he would have had to stay on the phone
through the day and into the night, making another
hundred calls at least. Old age isn't a battle; old age
is a massacre.

When he next went to the hospital for the annual
checkup on his carotids, the sonogram revealed that
the second carotid was now seriously obstructed
and required surgery. This would make the seventh
year in a row that he would have been hospitalized.
The news gave him a jolt—particularly as he'd heard
by phone that morning of Ezra Pollock's death—
but at least he would have the same vascular surgeon and the operation in the same hospital, and
this time he would know enough not to put up
with a local anesthetic and instead to ask to be un-
conscious throughout. He tried so hard to convince
himself from the experience of the first carotid surgery that there was nothing to worry about, he did
not bother to tell Nancy about the pending operation, especially while she still had her mother to tend
to. He did, however, make a determined effort to
locate Maureen Mrazek, though within only hours

he had exhausted any clues he might have had to her whereabouts.

That left Howie, whom by then he hadn't phoned in some time. It was as though once their parents were long dead all sorts of impulses previously proscribed or just nonexistent had been loosed in him, and his giving vent to them, in a sick man's rage—in the rage and despair of a joyless sick man unable to steer clear of prolonged illness's deadliest trap, the contortion of one's character—had destroyed the last link to the dearest people he'd known. His first love affair had been with his brother. The one solid thing throughout his life had been his admiration for this very good man. He'd made a mess of all his marriages, but throughout their adult lives he and his brother had been truly constant. Howie never had to be asked for anything. And now he'd lost him, and in the same way he'd lost Phoebe—by doing it to himself. As if there weren't already fewer and fewer people present who meant anything to him, he had completed the decomposition of the original family. But decomposing families was his specialty. Hadn't he robbed three children of a coherent childhood and the continuous loving protection of a father such as he himself had cherished, who had belonged exclusively to him and Howie, a father they and no one else had owned?

At the realization of all he'd wiped out, on his own and for seemingly no good reason, and what was still worse, against his every intention, *against his will*—of his harshness toward a brother who had never once been harsh to him, who'd never failed to soothe him and come to his aid, of the effect his leaving their households had had on his children— at the humiliating realization that not only physically had he now diminished into someone he did not want to be, he began striking his chest with his fist, striking in cadence with his self-admonition, and missing by mere inches his defibrillator. At that moment, he knew far better than Randy or Lonny ever could where he was insufficient. This ordinarily even-tempered man struck furiously at his heart like some fanatic at prayer, and, assailed by remorse not just for this mistake but for all his mistakes, all the ineradicable, stupid, inescapable mistakes— swept away by the misery of his limitations yet acting as if life's every incomprehensible contingency were of his making—he said aloud, "Without even Howie! To wind up like this, without even him!"

At Howie's ranch in Santa Barbara there was a comfortable guest cottage nearly as large as his condo. Years back he, Phoebe, and Nancy had stayed there for two weeks one summer while Howie and his family were vacationing in Europe. The pool was just outside the door, and Howie's horses were off in the hills, and the staff had made their meals and looked after them. Last he knew, one of Howie's kids—Steve, the oceanographer—was temporarily living there with a girlfriend. Did he dare to ask? Could he come right out and tell his brother that he'd like to stay at the guest house for a couple of months until he could figure out where and how to live next? If he could fly out to California after the surgery and enjoy his brother's company while beginning to recover . . .

He picked up the phone and dialed Howie. He got an answering machine and left his name and number. About an hour later he was called by Howie's youngest son, Rob. "My folks," Rob said, "are in Tibet." "Tibet? What are they doing in Tibet?" He believed they were in Santa Barbara and Howie just didn't want to take his call. "Dad went on business to Hong Kong, I believe to a board meeting, and my mother went with him. Then they went off to see Tibet." "Are Westerners allowed in Tibet?" he asked his nephew. "Oh, sure," Rob said. "They'll be gone another three weeks. Is there a message? I can e-mail them. That's what I've been doing when people call." "No, no need," he said. "How are all your brothers, Rob?" "Everybody's doing okay. How about you?" "I'm coming along," he said, and hung up.

Well, he was thrice divorced, a one-time serial husband distinguished no less by his devotion than by his misdeeds and mistakes, and he would have to continue to manage alone. From here on out he would have to manage everything alone. Even in his twenties, when he'd thought of himself as square, and on into his fifties, he'd had all the attention from women he could have wanted; from the time he'd entered art school it never stopped. It seemed as though he were destined for nothing else. But then something unforeseen happened, unforeseen and unpredictable: he had lived close to three quarters of a century, and the productive, active way of life was gone. He neither possessed the productive man's male allure nor was capable of germinating the masculine joys, and he tried not to long for them too much. On his own he had felt for a while that the missing component would somehow return to make him inviolable once again and reaffirm his mastery, that the entitlement mistakenly severed would be restored and he could resume where he'd left off only a few years before. But now it appeared that like any number of the elderly, he was in the process of becoming less and less and would have to see his aimless days through to the end as no more than what he was—the aimless days and the uncertain nights and the impotently putting up with the physical deterioration and the terminal sadness and the waiting and waiting for nothing. This is how it works out, he thought, this is what you could not know.

The man who swam the bay with Nancy's mother had arrived at where he'd never dreamed of being. It was time to worry about oblivion. It was the remote future.

One Saturday morning less than a week before the scheduled surgery—after a night of horrible dreaming when he'd awakened struggling to breathe at three A.M. and had to turn on all the lights in the apartment to calm his fears and was only able to fall

back to sleep with the lights still burning—he decided it would do him good to go to New York to
see Nancy and the twins and to visit Phoebe again,
who was now at home with a nurse. Normally his
deliberate independence constituted his bedrock
strength; it was why he could take up a new life in
a new place unconcerned over leaving friends and
family behind. But ever since he'd abandoned any
hope of living with Nancy or staying with Howie,
he felt himself turning into a childlike creature who
was weakening by the day. Was it the imminence of
the seventh annual hospitalization that was crushing his confidence? Was it the prospect of coming
steadily to be dominated by medical thoughts to
the exclusion of everything else? Or was it the realization that with each hospital stay, going back to
childhood and proceeding on up to his imminent
surgery, the number of presences at his bedside diminished and the army he'd begun with had dwindled to none? Or was it simply the foreboding of
helplessness to come?

What he had dreamed was that he was lying
naked beside Millicent Kramer, from his art class.
He was holding her cold dead body in bed the way
he'd held Phoebe the time the migraine had got so

bad that the doctor came to give her a morphine shot, which suppressed the pain but produced terrifying hallucinations. When he'd awakened in the night and turned on all the lights, he drank some water and threw open a window and paced the apartment to restore his stability, but despite himself he was thinking about only one thing: how it had been for her to kill herself. Did she do it in a rush, gobbling down the pills before she changed her mind? And after she'd finally taken them, did she scream that she didn't want to die, that she just couldn't face any more crippling pain, that all she wanted was for the pain to stop—scream and cry that all she wanted was for Gerald to be there to help her and to tell her to hang on and to assure her that she could bear it and that they were in it together? Did she die in tears, mumbling his name? Or did she do it all calmly, convinced at long last that she was not making a mistake? Did she take her time, contemplatively holding the pill bottle in her two hands before emptying the contents into her palm and slowly swallowing them with her last glass of water, with the last taste of water ever? Was she resigned and thoughtful, he wondered, courageous about everything she was leaving behind, perhaps smiling while she wept and remembered all the delights, all that had ever excited her and pleased her, her mind filled with hundreds of ordinary moments that meant little at the time but now seemed to have been especially intended to flood her days with commonplace bliss? Or had she lost interest in what she was leaving behind? Did she show no fear, thinking only, At last the pain is over, the pain is finally gone, and now I have merely to fall asleep to depart this amazing thing?

But how does one voluntarily choose to leave our fullness for that endless nothing? How would he do it? Could he lie there calmly saying goodbye? Had he Millicent Kramer's strength to eradicate everything? She was his age. Why not? In a bind like hers, what's a few years more or less? Who would dare to challenge her with leaving life precipitously? I must, I must, he thought, my six stents tell me I must one day soon fearlessly say goodbye. But leaving Nancy —I can't do it! The things that could happen to her on the way to school! His daughter left behind with no more of him for protection than their biological bond! And he bereft for eternity of her morning phone calls! He saw himself racing in every direction at once through downtown Elizabeth's main intersection—the unsuccessful father, the envious brother, the duplicitous husband, the helpless son —and only blocks from his family's jewelry store crying out for the cast of kin on whom he could not gain no matter how hard he pursued them. "Momma, Poppa, Howie, Phoebe, Nancy, Randy, Lonny—if only I'd known how to do it! Can't you hear me? I'm leaving! It's over and I'm leaving you all behind!" And those vanishing as fast from him as he from them turned just their heads to cry out in turn, and all too meaningfully, "Too late!"

Leaving—the very word that had conveyed him into breathless, panic-filled wakefulness, delivered alive from embracing a corpse.

He never made it to New York. Traveling north on the Jersey Turnpike, he remembered that just south of Newark Airport was the exit to the cemetery where his parents were buried, and when he reached there, he pulled off the turnpike and followed the road that twisted through a decrepit residential neighborhood and then past a grim old elementary school until it ended at a beat-up truck thoroughfare that bordered the five or so acres of Jewish cemetery. At the far end of the cemetery was a vacant street where driving instructors took their students to learn to make a U-turn. He edged the car slowly through the open, spiked gate and parked opposite a small building that must once have been a prayer house and was now a dilapidated, hollowed-out ruin. The synagogue that had administered the cemetery's affairs had been disbanded years ago when its congregants had moved to the Union, Essex, and Morris County suburbs, and it didn't look as if anyone was taking care of anything anymore. The earth was giving way and sinking around many of the graves, and footstones everywhere had tumbled onto their sides, and all this was not even in the original graveyard where his grandparents were buried, amid hundreds of darkened tombstones packed tightly together, but in the newer sections where the granite markers dated from the second half of the twentieth century. He had noticed none of this when they had assembled to bury his father. All he'd seen then was the casket resting on the belts that spanned the open grave. Plain and modest though it was, it took up the world. Then followed the brutality of the burial and the mouth full of dust.

In just the past month he had been among the

mourners at two funerals in two different cemeteries in Monmouth County, both rather less dreary
than this one, and less dangerous, too. During re-
cent decades, aside from vandals who damaged and
destroyed the stones and the outbuildings where
his parents were buried, there were muggers who
worked the cemetery as well. In broad daylight they
preyed upon the elderly who would occasionally
show up alone or in pairs to spend time visiting a
family gravesite. At his father's burial he had been informed by the rabbi that, if he was on his own, it
would be wisest to visit his mother and father during
the High Holy Day period, when the local police department, at the request of a committee of cemetery
chairmen, had agreed to provide protection for the
observant who turned out to recite the appropriate
psalms and remember their dead. He had listened to
the rabbi and nodded his head, but as he did not
number himself among the believers, let alone the
observant, and had a decided aversion to the High
Holy Days, he would never choose to come to the
cemetery then.

The dead were the two women in his class who'd
had cancer and who'd died within a week of each
other. There were many people from Starfish Beach

at these funerals. As he looked around he could not help speculating about who among them would be killed off next. Everyone thinks at some time or other that in a hundred years no one now alive will be on earth—the overwhelming force will sweep the place clean. But he was thinking in terms of days. He was musing like a marked man.

There was a short, plump elderly woman at both the funerals who wept so uncontrollably that she seemed more than a mere friend of the dead and instead, impossibly, the mother of both. At the second funeral, she stood and sobbed only a few feet from him and the overweight stranger next to him, who he assumed was her husband, even though (or perhaps because), with his arms crossed and his teeth clenched and his chin in the air, he remained strikingly aloof and apart from her, an indifferent spectator who refused any longer to put up with this person. If anything, her tears would seem to have aroused bitter contempt rather than sympathetic concern, because in the midst of the funeral, as the rabbi was intoning in English the words of the prayer book, the husband turned unbidden and impatiently asked, "You know why she's carrying on like that?" "I believe I do," he whispered back, meaning by this, It's because it is for her as it's been for me ever since I was a boy. It's because it is for her as it is for everyone. It's because life's most disturbing intensity is death. It's because death is so unjust. It's because once one has tasted life, death does not even seem natural. I had thought—*secretly I was certain*—that life goes on and on. "Well, you're wrong," the man said flatly, as though having read his mind. "She's like that all the time. That has been the story for fifty years," he added with an unforgiving scowl. "She's like that because she isn't eighteen anymore."

His parents were situated close to the perimeter of the cemetery, and it was a while before he found their graves by the iron fence that separated the last row of burial plots from a narrow side street that appeared to be a makeshift rest stop for truckers taking a break from their turnpike run. In the years since he'd last been here, he'd forgotten the effect the first sight of the headstone had on him. He saw their two names carved there, and he was incapacitated by the kind of sobbing that overpowers babies and leaves them limp. He elicited easily enough his last recollection of each of them—the hospital recollection—but when he tried to call up the earliest recollection, the effort to reach as far back as he could in their common past caused a second wave of feeling to overwhelm him.

They were just bones, bones in a box, but their bones were his bones, and he stood as close to the bones as he could, as though the proximity might link him up with them and mitigate the isolation born of losing his future and reconnect him with all that had gone. For the next hour and a half, those bones were the things that mattered most. They were all that mattered, despite the impingement of the neglected cemetery's environment of decay. Once he was with those bones he could not leave them, couldn't not talk to them, couldn't but listen to them when they spoke. Between him and those bones there was a great deal going on, far more than now transpired between him and those still clad in their flesh. The flesh melts away but the bones endure. The bones were the only solace there was to one who put no stock in an afterlife and knew without a doubt that God was a fiction and this was the only life he'd have. As young Phoebe might have put it back when they first met, it was not going too far to say that his deepest pleasure now was at the cemetery. Here alone contentment was attainable.

He did not feel as though he were playing at something. He did not feel as though he were trying to make something come true. This *was* what was true, this intensity of connection with those bones.

His mother had died at eighty, his father at ninety. Aloud he said to them, "I'm seventy-one. Your boy is seventy-one." "Good. You lived," his mother replied, and his father said, "Look back and atone for what you can atone for, and make the best of what you have left."

He couldn't go. The tenderness was out of control. As was the longing for everyone to be living. And to have it all all over again.

He was walking back through the cemetery to his car when he came upon a black man digging a grave with a shovel. The man was standing about two feet down in the unfinished grave and stopped shoveling and hurling the dirt out to the side as the visitor approached him. He wore dark coveralls and an old baseball cap, and from the gray in his mustache and the lines in his face he looked to be at least fifty. His frame, however, was still thick and strong.

"I thought they did this with a machine," he said to the gravedigger.

"In big cemeteries, where they do many graves, a lot of times they use machines, that's right." He spoke like a Southerner, but very matter-of-factly, very precisely, more like a pedantic schoolteacher than a physical laborer. "I don't use a machine," the gravedigger continued, "because it can sink the other graves. The soil can give and it can crush in on the box. And you have the gravestones you have to deal with. It's just easier in my case to do everything by hand. Much neater. Easier to take the dirt away without ruining anything else. I use a real small tractor that I can maneuver easily, and I dig by hand."

Now he noticed the tractor in the grassy pathway between the graves. "The tractor's for what?"

"Use that to haul the dirt away. I've been doing it long enough that I know how much dirt to take away and how much dirt to leave. The first ten trailers of dirt I take away. Whatever's left I throw up on boards. I put down plywood boards. You can see 'em. I lay down three plywood boards so the dirt doesn't sit on the grass itself. The last half of the dirt I throw out onto the boards. To fill in afterwards. Then I cover everything with this green carpet. Try to make it nice for the family. So it looks like grass."

"How do you dig it? Mind if I ask?"

"Nope," said the gravedigger, still a couple feet down, standing where he'd been digging. "Most folks don't care. With most folks, the less they know the better."

"I want to know," he assured him. And he did. He did not want to go.

"Well, I have a map. Shows every grave that's ever been sold or laid out in the cemetery. With the map you locate the plot, purchased who knows when, fifty years ago, seventy-five years ago. Once I got it located I come here with a probe. There it is. That seven-foot spike on the ground. I take this probe and I go down two or three feet, and that's how I locate the next grave over. Bang—you hit it and you hear it. And then I take a stick and I mark on the ground where the new grave is. Then I have a wood frame that I lay down on the ground and that's what I cut the soil to. I take an edger first and

I cut the sod to the size of the frame. Then I size it down, make one-foot-square pieces of sod, and put them back of the grave, out of sight—because I don't want to make any kind of mess where the funeral will be. The less dirt, the easier it is to clean up. I don't ever want to leave a mess. I lay down a board back of the grave next to it, where I can carry the squares of sod to it on the fork. I lay 'em like a grid so it looks like where I took 'em out. That takes about an hour. It's a hard part of the job. Once I've done that, then I dig. I bring the tractor over, and my trailer attached. What I do is, I dig first. That's what I'm doing now. My son digs the hard part. He's stronger than I am now. He likes to come in after I'm done. When he's busy or not around I dig the whole thing myself. But when he's here I always let him dig the harder part. I'm fifty-eight. I don't dig like I used to. When he started I had him here all the time, and we'd take turns digging. That was fun because he was young and it gave me time to talk to him, just the two of us alone."

"What did you talk to him about?"

"Not about graveyards," he said, laughing hard. "Not like I'm talking to you."

"What then?"

"Things in general. Life in general. Anyway, I dig the first half. I use two shovels, a square shovel when the digging is easy and you can take more dirt, and then I use just a round pointed shovel, just a standard shovel. That's what you use for basic digging, a regular common shovel. If it's easy digging, especially in the spring when the ground isn't real solid, when the ground is wet, I use the big shovel and I can take out big shovelfuls and heave 'em into the trailer. I dig front to back, and I dig a grid, and as I go I use my edger to square the hole. I use that and a straight fork—they call it a spading fork. I use that to edge too, to bang down, cut the edges, and keep it square. You've got to keep it square as you go. The first ten loads go into the trailer and I take it over to an area in the cemetery where it's low and where we're filling that area, and I dump the trailer, come back, fill it up again. Ten loads. At that point I'm about halfway. That's about three foot."

"So from start to finish, how long does it take?"

"It'll take about three hours to do my end. Could even take four hours. Depends on the dig. My son's a good digger—takes him about two and a half hours more. It's a day's work. I usually come in about six in the morning, and my son comes in around ten. But he's busy now and I tell him he can do it when he wants. If the weather's hot, he'll come at night when it's cooler. With Jewish people we only get a day's notice, and we got to do it quick. At the Christian cemetery"—he pointed to the large, sprawling cemetery that lay across the road—"the undertakers will give us two or three days' notice."

"And you been doing this work how long?"

"Thirty-four years. A long time. It's good work. It's peaceful. Gives you time to think. But it's a lot of work. Starting to hurt my back. One day soon I'm turning it all over to my son. He'll take over and I'm moving back to where it's warm year round. Because, don't forget, I only told you about digging it. You got to come back and fill it up. That takes you three hours. Put the sod back, and so on. But let's go back to when the grave is dug. My son has finished up. He's squared it up, it's flat on the bottom. It's six foot deep, it looks good, you could jump down in the hole. Like the old guy used to say who I first dug with, it's got to be flat enough to lay a bed out on it. I used to laugh at him when he said that. But it's so: you've got this hole, six foot deep, and it's got to be right for the sake of the family and right for the sake of the dead."

"Mind if I stand here and watch?"

"Not at all. This is nice diggin'. No rocks. Straight in."

He watched him dig down with the shovel and then hoist up the dirt and heave it easily onto the plywood. Every few minutes he would use the tines of the fork to loosen up the sides and then choose one of the two shovels to resume the digging. Once in a while a small rock would strike the plywood, but mostly what came up out of the grave was moist brown soil that broke apart easily on leaving the shovel.

He was watching from beside the gravestone to the rear of which the gravedigger had laid out the square patches of sod that he would return to the plot after the funeral. The sod was fitted perfectly to the piece of plywood on which the patches rested. And still he did not want to go, not while by merely turning his head he could catch a glimpse of his parents' stone. He never wanted to go.

Pointing to the gravestone, the gravedigger said, "This guy here fought in World War Two. Prisoner of war in Japan. Helluva nice guy. Know him from when he used to come visit his wife. Nice guy. Always a decent guy. Got stuck with your car, the kind of guy who'd pull you out."

"So you know some of these people."

"Sure I do. There's a boy here, seventeen. Killed in a car crash. His friends come by and put beer cans on his grave. Or a fishing pole. He liked to fish."

He cleaned a clump of dirt from his shovel by banging it down on the plywood and then resumed digging. "Oops," he said, looking out across the cemetery to the street, "here she comes," and he instantly put aside the shovel and pulled off his soiled yellow work gloves. For the first time he stepped up out of the grave and banged each of his battered work shoes against the other to dislodge the dirt that was clinging to them.

An elderly black woman was approaching the open grave carrying a small plaid cooler in one hand and a thermos in the other. She was wearing running shoes, a pair of nylon slacks the color of the gravedigger's work gloves, and a blue, zippered New York Yankees team jacket.

The gravedigger said to her, "This is a nice gentleman who's been visiting with me this morning."

She nodded and handed him the cooler and the thermos, which he set down beside his tractor.

"Thank you, honey. Arnold still sleeping?"

"He's up," she said. "I made you two meat loaf and one baloney."

"That's good. Thank you."

She nodded again and then turned and went out of the cemetery, where she got into her car and drove away.

"That your wife?" he asked the gravedigger.

"That is Thelma." Smiling, he added, "She nourishes me."

"She isn't your mother."

"Oh, no, no—no, sir," said the gravedigger with a laugh, "not Thelma."

"And she doesn't mind coming out here?"

"You gotta do what you gotta do. That's her philosophy in a nutshell. What it comes down to for Thelma is just diggin' a hole. This is nothing special to her."

"You want to eat your lunch, so I'm going to leave you. But I want to ask—I wonder if you dug my parents' graves. They're buried over here. Let me show you."

The gravedigger followed him a ways until they could see clearly the site of his family stone.

"Did you dig those?" he asked him.

"Sure, I did them," the gravedigger said.

"Well, I want to thank you. I want to thank you for everything you've told me and for how clear you've been. You couldn't have made things more concrete. It's a good education for an older person. I thank you for the concreteness, and I thank you for being so careful and considerate when you dug my parents' graves. I wonder if I might give you something."

"I received my fee at the time, thank you."

"Yes, but I'd like to give you something for you and your son. My father always said, 'It's best to give while your hand is still warm.'" He slipped him two fifties, and as the gravedigger's large, roughened palm closed around the bills, he looked at him closely, at the genial, creased face and the pitted skin of the mustached black man who might some-day soon be digging a hole for him that was flat enough at the bottom to lay a bed on.

In the days that followed he had only to yearn for them to conjure them up, and not merely the bone

parents of the aging man but the flesh parents of
the boy still in bud, off to the hospital on the bus
with *Treasure Island* and *Kim* in the bag his mother
balanced on her knees. A boy still in bud but because of her presence showing no fear and shoving
aside all his thoughts about the bloated body of
the seaman that he'd watched the Coast Guard remove from the edge of the oil-clotted beach.

He went in early on a Wednesday morning for
the surgery on his right carotid artery. The routine
was exactly as it had been for the surgery on the left
carotid. He waited his turn in the anteroom with
everyone else on the surgical schedule until his name
was called, and in his flimsy gown and paper slippers he was accompanied by a nurse into the operating room. This time when he was asked by the
masked anesthesiologist if he wanted the local or
the general anesthetic, he requested the general so
as to make the surgery easier to bear than it had
been the first time around.

The words spoken by the bones made him feel
buoyant and indestructible. So did the hard-won
subjugation of his darkest thoughts. Nothing could
extinguish the vitality of that boy whose slender little torpedo of an unscathed body once rode the big

Atlantic waves from a hundred yards out in the wild ocean all the way in to shore. Oh, the abandon of it, and the smell of the salt water and the scorching sun! Daylight, he thought, penetrating everywhere, day after summer day of that daylight blazing off a living sea, an optical treasure so vast and valuable that he could have been peering through the jeweler's loupe engraved with his father's initials at the perfect, priceless planet itself—at his home, the billion-, the trillion-, the quadrillion-carat planet Earth! He went under feeling far from felled, anything but doomed, eager yet again to be fulfilled, but nonetheless, he never woke up. Cardiac arrest. He was no more, freed from being, entering into nowhere without even knowing it. Just as he'd feared from the start.

ABOUT THE AUTHOR

In 1997 Philip Roth won the Pulitzer Prize for *American Pastoral*. In 1998 he received the National Medal of Arts at the White House and in 2002 the highest award of the American Academy of Arts and Letters, the Gold Medal in Fiction, previously awarded to John Dos Passos, William Faulkner, and Saul Bellow, among others. He has twice won the National Book Award, the PEN/Faulkner Award, and the National Book Critics Circle Award.

In 2005 *The Plot Against America* received the Society of American Historians' prize for "the outstanding historical novel on an American theme for 2003–2004." In the United Kingdom it won the W. H. Smith Award for the Best Book of the Year, making Roth the first writer in the forty-six-year history of the prize to win it twice.

In 2005 Roth also became the third living American writer to have his work published in a comprehensive, definitive edition by the Library of America. The last of the eight volumes is scheduled for publication in 2013.